What people are saying about

The Unexpected

Shakespeare told the most enduring, fascinating, timeless and gripping stories. Over the centuries they have been adapted and performed in countless innovative ways. James Hartley has, in these adaptations, retold the Bard's words in language that will captivate children.

Christopher Ecclestone

READER REV

T0306439

This Middle Grade/YA sci-fi Shakespearean retelling is reminiscent of a Rick Riordan book with a touch of Orson Scott Card's sci-fi vibes. I really loved the immersion that this novel garnered, courtesy of the spectacular worldbuilding. In fact, I think my favorite part about *The Unexpected* is the way it sucked me in and made me interested in a plot that I initially didn't think I would like very much. That's good writing!

Audrey Laurence

The Shakespeare's Moon series of books for young teenage readers are about children who get mixed up in the plots of Shakespeare's plays. Aimed at helping children and teenagers approach the worlds of Shakespeare's plays in a fresh, imaginative new way, the plays allow readers to see the plays from the inside. This third installation in the series brings with it a feast to your imagination. It's a fun and lovable read which is targeted toward the younger (pre-teen/teen) reader, but does not disappoint even the most adult mind. The kind of book, and series that makes you sit back and think - "huh, so that's what it all meant"

Melanie Laing

A well written, third instalment of Shakespeare retellings set within a school environment. It works as a stand alone, but character development is seen best when reading all of them. Perfect for those who love Shakespeare and as an introduction to ease some reluctant student's into the Bard's literary world.

Han Hunter

The series uses 3 of Shakespeare's well known works (Macbeth, Romeo and Juliet, and Julius Caesar) in such an interesting and innovative way... The Unexpected was a great ending to a good series. I would recommend it to many casual Shakespeare fans and to teens who want something a little different.

Jennifer Noble

The Unexpected

Shakespeare's Moon Act III

The Unexpected

Shakespeare's Moon Act III

James Hartley

LODESTONE
BOOKS

Winchester, UK
Washington, USA

JOHN HUNT PUBLISHING

First published by Lodestone Books, 2020
Lodestone Books is an imprint of John Hunt Publishing Ltd., No. 3 East Street,
Alresford, Hampshire SO24 9EE, UK
office@jhpbooks.net
www.johnhuntpublishing.com

For distributor details and how to order please visit the 'Ordering' section on our website.

Text copyright: James Hartley 2018

ISBN: 978 1 78904 294 8
978 1 78904 295 5 (ebook)
Library of Congress Control Number: 2018964467

A CIP catalogue record for this book is available from the British Library.

Design: Stuart Davies

UK: Printed and bound by CPI Group (UK) Ltd, Croydon, CR0 4YY
US: Printed and bound by Thomson-Shore, 7300 West Joy Road, Dexter, MI 48130

We operate a distinctive and ethical publishing philosophy in
all areas of our business, from our global network of authors to
production and worldwide distribution.

For Seets and Matty
You came. You saw. You conquered.

Please Note: This book talks a lot about *Vercingetorix Throws Down His Arms at the Feet of Julius Caesar* by Lionel Noel Royer (1899). You might want to Google it and have a look and see if you know anyone in it before you read.

Imagination is more important than knowledge.
Knowledge is limited.
Imagination encircles the world.

Albert Einstein

I

Late February, 44 NE (New Era)
St Francis' School. Old England.

"At last," said Athy Jull-Costa, dropping the net curtains back into place. "The Martians have landed."

The *Giraffe*, a sleek, teardrop-shaped cruiser, was sitting in a rising cloud of dust on the school's front lawn. Beyond it lay a line of jagged tree stumps while up above, in the dirty brown sky, a huge, low Moon stared down like a spotlight, impossibly close.

Two children jumped out through the cruiser's silver wall. They were brother and sister; the boy dark-haired, thin and almost as tall as his pale sibling despite being two years younger. Both were wearing short-distance breathing helmets which flickered with rainbows as they ran across to and then through the protective screen at the school's main entrance.

The *Giraffe*'s thrusters whirred and a fresh cloud of black earth billowed up beneath its silver hull. The cruiser tipped sharply upwards to point clear of the spiked trees. Dead leaves spraying out in every direction disintegrated before they reached the school buildings.

Alice, the girl from space, was picking flecks of dirt off her brother's white travel suit. Neither she nor Charlie had eyebrows but otherwise they might have been Earthlings. "This place is even worse than I thought it would be!" she was saying. "Did you see the colour of the sky? It looks nothing like the sims!"

"And the Moon?" Charlie replied, widening his eyes. "So close?"

"That has to be the pollution," Alice decided.

"Good afternoon, you two," came an elderly voice from above their heads. Mrs Jull-Costa, looking down over the bannisters, gave them a friendly wave. "Yoo hoo!"

"Wow she looks like Grandma Red," Charlie whispered as they craned their necks to look up.

"Of course she does," Alice answered. "What did you expect?"

"Leave your suits and helmets in the porch by the door," the old lady called out.

Charlie ran ahead of his sister up the creaking stairs. Mrs Jull-Costa was waiting on the top landing, her face lit by dusty, yellow light. She was wearing strange clothes, rubbing her hands, stooped but alert. Her eyes were Pacific blue and seemed to belong to someone else, someone who lived inside the wrinkly, grey body.

"You look just like our great-grandma," Charlie told her, as direct as always. "She's called Granny Red."

"Hello, miss," Alice began, puffed out from the climb. She stuck out a hand as her mother had told her to. "We're Charlie and Alice."

"Of course you are."

Two black and white cats, tails spiked upwards, weaved in and out of Mrs Jull-Costa's ankles, mewling. "Come closer, my dears, so I can have a proper look at you. You must be so tired after all that travelling." The sight of the two of them made the old lady's hands tremble. The children walked across and hugged her. "My, how you've grown up! We've had no word – no word at all – for the last year or so."

Charlie's eyes went wide and he threw up his arms. "It was impossible to communicate, miss. All the Coms were down! The storms on Mars have been terrible, miss."

"Athy, please. Or Aunt Athy, if you must. The people here call me Ma'am Athy – that's the protocol, but I think you both should call me Aunt Athy. Just not 'miss': whatever you call me, don't call me 'miss'."

"The storms were really bad, Aunt Athy." Alice's shoulder-length dark-blonde hair, the colour of drying sand, was held back by a glowing pink band. "That's why Mum said we had to come here. They took us all up to a big space station orbiting Mars but Mum said even that might have to be evacuated soon."

"Your mother is well, is she? That's good to know."

"Your sister is still alive, too," Charlie said, almost absentmindedly. He chewed a fingernail, up on tiptoes, as he peered out of the small, grilled window. Down below was the black lawn and sharp tree stumps. The sky was the colour of fudge, some leaves and debris still to settle. "Grandma Red is your sister, isn't she, miss? I mean, Aunty?"

"We call your sister Grandma Red," Alice explained. "Oh! Which reminds me. Charlie – where's the thing Granny Red gave you? For Aunty Athy?"

Charlie began searching the pockets of his travelling overalls. "Oh, yeah. Hmm. Where did I put it?"

"I'm afraid they took everything else we had at customs on the Moon, but we did manage to hide the most important thing."

"Are you really, like, a hundred and twenty years old?" Charlie asked Athy, holding up a locket the size of a walnut.

"Thereabouts," answered their great-aunt, eyes fixed on the brassy droplet the boy was passing to her.

"Alice hid that in her mouth when they were searching us," Charlie explained, clearly impressed with his sister. "They said they were worried we were going to be infected or something so they took everything else we had."

Mrs Jull-Costa stared at the locket for so long Alice shuffled to her side and said: "Grandma said to give it to you, Aunty Athy. She said you'd understand."

"Wow! The Moon is even more massive from here," Charlie cooed.

"Of course I understand," whispered Mrs Jull-Costa, rubbing the locket between her palms. She placed a hand on the girl's head. "It's from my sister Kizzie. Your great-grandmother. Grandma Red, you said you call her, wasn't it? Yes, I do understand. I do indeed. It belonged to both of us, this little locket did."

"Is this a real school, Aunt Athy?" Charlie called out, still on tiptoes at the window. "Or, like a museum or something? To show people what schools were like in the olden times?" The Moon seemed so close he could make out the ashy buildings of the New Lunar Colonies on the nearside surface. "It's, like, so *zambliny*." 'Zamblin' was a Martian word for a small unit of time. Charlie meant 'tiny' or 'quaint'.

Mrs Jull-Costa took a deep breath as though she were coming up from underwater. "My dears, you must be tired. Something to eat and drink, perhaps? These are my rooms, here. Come along inside."

The old lady used her index finger to unlock a panelled door on the corridor wall and the three of them entered a large, shadowy attic with a sloping roof. On one side of the main room was a sofa covered with so many hairs it looked like an animal itself. The two cats leapt up on to it, mewling louder than ever.

"Oh, those two are hungry are usual," Mrs Jull-Costa said, shuffling across to a small kitchen area, waving for the light to come on. "Aren't you, Romulus and Remus?"

Alice didn't like the smell of the room. After the cleanliness and control of Mars and the Space Stations – even the Moon had been clean – the old lady's flat ponged something terrible. Cats and damp. Alice felt she could almost take a bite out of the thick, stinky air.

Charlie ran across the floor and lifted the curtain of a window in the furthest wall. He looked out at a huge diamond-coloured dome which shimmered through the dirty sky. Although he was used to domes, he'd never seen one so large and bright. "Wow! Is *that* the school, Aunty?" he asked, turning, beaming. "I mean, the *real* school?"

"Yes. Very good, young man. There are some classrooms dotted about and a few other spaces under the ground linked by tunnels but that's the main dome, yes."

"Are we going to sleep up here, Aunty?" Alice asked, unable

to hide the worry in her voice. She looked at the panelled walls. Even they seemed rather greasy. "It's so old! I've never seen rooms like this in real life."

"No, Alice. I don't think you'll be allowed to sleep up here. They won't allow it."

"Who's 'they', Aunty?"

The old lady turned to look at Alice, thought about speaking, but decided against it. "You'll find out soon enough." She pulled open an old-fashioned fridge and the light inside lit up every wrinkle on her face and a few hairs on her chin. "You've come at a rather turbulent time in the school's history, I'm afraid, my dear. Storms here also, of another kind, sadly. Turbulence and change everywhere."

"Can we go outside, Aunty-A?" Charlie asked, running back across the room in his socks. He came to a skidding halt beside his sister and bumped into her, ignoring her whine of complaint. "I want to play sports outside, in the open air. That was the best thing about living here, Mum and Dad said."

"Oh, I'm afraid you won't be able to do that at the moment, Charlie. I'm sure you'll have both noticed the rather unhealthy colour of the sky. It's far too dangerous to go outside these days. They say it might not be right again for some time."

Charlie, momentarily sad, was cheered by the sight of the plates of food his great-aunt had unwrapped and placed on the sideboard in front of them. She told them to pull up a stool and, as the children ate and chatted, Athy, clutching the brass locket they'd brought from her sister on Mars, wandered into her small bathroom and stood in the darkness, remembered when Kizzie had been here at school with her.

It could have been yesterday.

II

Wake up, Athy. Wake up…

I'm still not sure if Kizzie planned everything that day. How could she know if the magic would work or not?

She was my older sister and I trusted her. I was weak, homesick, too young to be able to know what was going on. Nine years old, I was shy and easy prey for bullies. I cried a lot. I couldn't say what I felt. I don't know if I can, even now. But I remember. I remember that day perfectly.

Athy, wake up. It's time…

I remember it was cold that morning, so cold the blankets on the bed felt like they were wet. My breath was steaming as I stood in the blue darkness. It was early in the morning, before dawn, just before Christmas.

Don't worry, Athy. Put your clothes on over your nightie.

In those days the doors were all locked from inside and it was easy to get out. We went down the back stairs to where a corridor from the dining room led to the main hall. There was a bathroom in the corridor and Kizzie opened a small window in one of the cubicles. I stood on the cistern and crawled out into an icy morning. The sky, I remember, was turning pale pink above the shadows of tree heads. There was no birdsong. The frost crunched underfoot. The top layer of snow was hard but under was soft and my shoes sank. Kizzie put her finger to her lips and led me down the main path.

Ssh. Follow me.

The world is a different place before dawn. I saw birds asleep, curled up in black balls with their heads buried under their wings as though hiding. The sky, slowly appearing, pink, was very clear, as though it had been scratched clean by the night. The Moon was half-undercover, trying to sleep. Venus twinkled, between heaven and Earth.

I followed Kizzie, not knowing where we were going. Later she told me she'd listened to me the night before, crying, lost again, and had decided to do something about it. *I'll cheer you up*, she'd thought.

Kizzie had always been good to me, always looked after me. My father sometimes said it wasn't good for me, that I needed to stand on my own two feet, but I had never been as confident as Kizzie was. She seemed to know what to say, and could speak and mix well with people. I was quiet and nothing came easily for me. I tried drawing, dancing and playing the piano, all of which I did badly: I really couldn't do anything well. The only thing I really liked was art. Pictures. Paintings. Looking at books of paintings. Writing about them.

Climb under the fence. Be careful with the nettles.

As we crossed the boundary, leaving the school grounds, I felt worried for the first time. The light was changing, the sun stretching its bright arms. We were out in the open. I remember the ice crystals hanging off the pavilion roof sparkling, dripping. The fields and hills were covered with a ghostly mist which the light chased away. Leaves lay in our path hard and sprayed with icing sugar.

Where are we going, Kizzie?

Sshh. Just keep going, Athy. Follow me. Stop worrying!

A little further down the path Kizzie stopped me and pointed at a great oak tree in the middle of a meadow we were passing.

There. That's it.

The oak was imperious in the dawn light. It was the biggest tree for miles around, inspiring and eerie as the sun rose directly behind its mighty trunk.

The oak was older than the anyone who lived in the village, older than most of the houses, older, perhaps, than the school, Kizzie said, as we crunched through the long grass towards it. We walked in its shadow, golden sunbeams firing out either side of us.

Trees, especially oaks, have always been magical, Kizzie said.

And I did feel the magic then. Perhaps that was part of it: that I had to believe. My sister was one of those people who made you believe magic existed. She was so convinced, you couldn't not feel something too.

Isn't it beautiful, Athy?

It is, it is.

At the foot of the oak, Kizzie bowed her head and I saw her lips moving but I heard no words. It seemed only right to say a prayer: I mumbled a *Hail Mary* or an *Our Father*, not really knowing why. They were the only prayers I knew.

I saw Kizzie press something, paper perhaps, folded paper, into a cubbyhole in the trunk. She bowed her head, hiss-whispered and turned to me.

Take this, Athy.

I looked at what Kizzie was holding out to me. It was a brassy, golden locket on a chain.

Open it.

It was opened by a brass button on the side. The button sprang a door which revealed, inside, a small portrait of the *Mona Lisa*, the painting by Leonardo da Vinci.

Take the painting out.

I did so, my hands cold, my breath smoking.

Read the poem.

On the back of the portrait, I read, in Kizzie's handwriting:

Bathed in full moonlight
This locket alight,
Thrice life becomes Art;
Thrice Art becomes Life.

Kizzie helped me fold the note, reset the picture and put her hand over mine, her eyes closed, as we both pressed the locket closed. I felt the warmth of her hands flow through my own and, perhaps it was my imagination, but I also thought I felt the locket glow.

Do you understand?

I think so.

When there is a full Moon hold this locket up to its light, say those words and you can go into your pictures, Athy. When the world gets too much for you, go there. Live in your dreams, in your imagination. Go somewhere you love and come back stronger.

We turned back to the school, away from the tree, and I saw the turrets and red roofs of the main building poking up from behind the pointed top of the snowy trees. The sky was a high, perfect blue, and life felt better, though I didn't really understand what I'd been shown.

The last thing I remember about that morning was looking back at the mighty oak when we got to the path. It was black and skeletal against the bright ball of the rising sun, almost too bright to look at, our snowy footprints cutting two paths from it to us. The sun's blinding light spangled through the branches and I put my hand to my brow to better see it and bowed slightly.

Thank you, I said, in my mind, to the tree.

And this seemed to please it. All its darkness seemed, just for a moment, to soften.

III

Athy, Aunt Athy! Please! Wake up!

Alice and Charlie took turns to tug on their aunt's cardigan. Behind them a dark-robed figure dominated the doorway, a teacher who had identified himself as Mr Chor-Zor, the Biotech Master. This man's skin was very smooth: he had the look of a coffee-coloured mannequin. As both children knew, this was because he was a modified, or mod.

Modifieds were machines. Their skin was synthetic, their very realistic features, voices and movements generated by technology hidden inside their bare, shiny skulls. They could change how they looked at will though most, out of respect for the fact that humans couldn't do the same, created a single 'face', which they called an *aspect*, and kept to it. Mr Chor-Zor's *aspect* was a plainly handsome man of about forty. It was an *aspect* intended to convey seriousness, strength and power.

"What's wrong?" Athy asked, turning and slipping the locket into her skirts when she saw the caped figure in the doorway. "Ah, Mr Chor-Zor! Good evening."

"May I enter?" asked Chor-Zor. He was wearing a modern all-in-one suit as dark as his flowing cape. Human teachers wore white suits and capes while mods tended to wear browns and blacks.

"Of course, of course." Mrs Jull-Costa presented her great-niece and nephew by name and as Chor-Zor shook their hands his face almost showed a smile. Neither Charlie nor Alice were particularly fazed by the sight of the teacher: cyborgs, modifieds and robot assistants (RAs) were common on the Moon, Mars and the Space Stations.

Chor-Zor stood in the centre of the room, gloved hands crossed in front of his body. Romulus and Remus, upright on the sofa, bristled from nose to tail. "I came to ask you, Ma'am Athy, if you were part of the illegal celebrations which took place this morning?"

Mrs Jull-Costa furrowed her brow. "I'm sorry?"

"Ma'am Mallowan returned to the school earlier today and there were people celebrating in the tunnels and dome. These celebrations seemed organised and some took place during class time. As you know, this is against protocol and, with the situation as delicate as it is, such breaches could have quite a serious effect on school morale."

"Oh, Mrs Mallowan is back, is she? I didn't know."

"A simple return to school is no cause for celebration."

The children couldn't help looking confused: they had no idea what the argument was about. Their aunt had walked across to the centre of the room to stand directly in front of the much taller, broader figure of Chor-Zor. Alice guessed Mrs – or Ma'am – Mallowan might be the Headmistress of St Francis'. She seemed to remember her mother mentioning the name. Or perhaps she'd read it?

"I'm confused about something, sir." Mrs Jull-Costa crossed her arms. "How could I have celebrated if I didn't even know Mrs Mallowan was coming back today?"

"There was a commotion on the front lawn. Your name came up in the log: you opened the front door seals."

"I opened the seals for these two youngsters. I booked the landing slot."

"You should have alerted the Reception Committee. You are aware of the protocol. There was no logical reason for any divergence."

"Oh, this is tosh," was the old lady's answer, foot tapping. "They're here, they arrived, that's all there is to it." The cats jumped down off the sofa and began prowling around Athy's ankles, hissing.

"Protocol clearly states," Chor-Zor began, going on to list the rules pertaining to the reception of students arriving by spaceship from the New Lunar Colonies, any orbiting Space Stations or Mars.

"Consider them received, Mr Chor-Zor," Mrs Jull-Costa said, when the mod finally finished. "I will fill in the records as soon as the children are fed and watered. Surely you have more important business to attend to?"

"Indeed, I do." Mr Chor-Zor pointed at Charlie, his gloves squeaking. "Following protocol, the boy will be roomed in ST-33, the girl in ST-5, for Quarantine. I will escort them down myself."

"How very polite of you," sniffed Mrs Jull-Costa. She nodded towards Charlie and Alice, surprising them by changing – softening – her voice. "You'll have to go with Mr Chor-Zor, my dears. The rules state that you must be taken to special sleeping quarters for tonight at least. It's for the good of everyone."

"When will we see you again?" Alice asked. She had a hairpin in her mouth and was pulling a ponytail into a knot.

"Soon," her great-aunt replied, with a sad but reassuring smile.

"Are we going to the dome?" asked Charlie. He walked across to his shoes and kick-slipped them on.

"No," answered Chor-Zor. "Your temporary accommodation will be in the Subterranean Sector, located adjacent to the dome but not forming any part of it. Until you have passed through quarantine neither of you will be allowed into the dome. Your movement will be restricted until you are proven to be disease and risk free, as protocol dictates."

"Quarantine," sighed Alice, blowing up her fringe. "Again?"

"All Martians are required, by protocol, to serve three weeks' quarantine. Due to your screening at the NLCs this is reduced to a mandatory twenty-four hours."

"We only went down to the surface of Mars once, sir," protested Charlie. "Most of the time we were on the orbiting Stations."

"And they're *way* cleaner than this place," added Alice. "No offence, Aunty."

"Just do as Mr Chor-Zor says," their aunt said, rubbing Charlie's unruly hair and leaning down to kiss Alice on the top of her head. "So lovely to see you. You really don't know how much good it's done me."

"On account of the coming storm," Chor-Zor went on, turning again to Athy, "it has been decided to evacuate all non-sealable areas and to use pre-saved air. You are thus advised that it is considered unsafe to stay in the main building. This is the opinion of the Magistrate. Your apartments should be evacuated immediately." He pointed a metallic finger at Romulus and Remus. "And I should also remind you that these creatures are a grave health hazard..."

"Good afternoon, Mr Chor-Zor," said Athy. "Please leave my rooms now."

Alice waved at her aunt as she followed the caped teacher out. "See you soon, Aunty."

"Goodbye, my dears."

The panelled door shimmered into place with Athy on one side and Chor-Zor, Alice and Charlie on the other.

"Is there really going to be a storm, sir?" Alice asked as the three of them began down the staircase. Only the children's feet made any sound on the stairs. Chor-Zor used air-pads and so descended silently.

"Yes."

"A bad one?" asked Charlie.

"One of the worst this planet has ever seen."

"Maybe *we* should ask Aunt Athy to leave?" Alice asked, as they came to the bottom of the stairs. "If it's not safe?" They were in the main hall where they had arrived. It was grey and quiet and it took them a moment to notice a very tall, thin lady standing in front of the fireplace watching them. She stepped forwards like a moving shadow.

"Oh, there's little point in doing that, children," the grey lady cooed. "Your great-aunt will do whatever she wants, I'm sure – just as she always does." She poked out a long white hand. "I'm Ma'am Mallowan, Headmistress of St Francis' School. And you must be Ma'am Athy's great-grandnephew and grandniece?"

"Hello," said Charlie, slightly shocked at the thin, stern-faced woman. She looked as old as their great-aunt but far fiercer.

Chor-Zor was staring at the floor.

"And you must be Alice," Ma'am Mallowan went on. "May I take this opportunity to welcome you both to St Francis."

"Nice to meet you," Alice managed.

Mrs Mallowan seemed to be made of steel; a cold, grey metal rod lit up by the diamond-blue shine-spots of her eyes. A thin, pink line of lipstick surrounded her unsmiling mouth.

All turned at the noise of a door opening behind them. A moment later a tall modified teacher came stomping around the corner. This mod's skin was a dull, red-black colour and she had a long, plaited ponytail – copper red – which bounced down the length of her back. Her facial features were almost silver, cogwheel eyes and a shining mouth, and her *aspect* was quite the most stunning Alice or Charlie had ever seen. Alice thought her beautiful and Charlie stared up at her – enveloped in the cloud of smoky, musky perfume which wafted off her cape – in a kind of daze.

"Ms Row-Lin," the Headmistress said, with the barest bow of her head. "What an unexpected surprise."

"I'm here for the meeting, Ma'am," Row-Lin replied, curtseying. She turned and acknowledged Chor-Zor with a quick bow. "I hope I'm not late."

"You should also come to the meeting," Mrs Mallowan told Chor-Zor. "It's to determine protocol for the storm this evening."

"I must take the children to quarantine," Chor-Zor replied.

Mrs Mallowan arched her eyebrows as she thought about this reply. She crooked an arm and stroked her nose with a finger. "Very well. But be as quick as you can, there's no time to lose."

Chor-Zor grunted and bowed. "Ma'am."

"We'll be in the Eleusinian Room," Mrs Mallowan said, leading Row-Lin away. "Goodbye, children."

"Goodbye!"

"Follow," Chor-Zor barked, setting off, and Charlie and Alice did as they were told. They crossed the hall and on turning the corner found themselves at a double-sealed security screen. This, once Chor-Zor dissolved it, opened on to the top of a wide staircase which led down to a well-lit underground tunnel. "Walk on. Walk on."

The sky they could see through the transparent tunnel roof was coming night, black and muggy but for the huge disc of the Moon. Clouds passed as they watched, wispy as smoke, sometimes colliding with the transparent material of the tunnel roof to leave brown smudges and dripping, yellow stains. Alice wrinkled her nose and made a face at Charlie. He nodded to show he felt the same: this wasn't the gorgeous, blue paradise they'd been told about in school and at home.

At the end of the tunnel was a flickering reception area lined with three turnstiles. The St Francis' badge and various smiling faces, human, cyborg and modified, looked down at them from moving 3-D screens. Chor-Zor made a sign to show he wanted the children to enter a turnstile each. Alice and Charlie both noticed dark glass boxes on either side of them, buried in the corridor walls, and knew they were being watched.

Entering his turnstile, a voice told Charlie to stretch out his arms and legs. He could see his sister doing the same in the next booth. A beam of red light passed from her hair and traced its way down her arms to her hands and legs. A green light zapped once somewhere up above them both and the doors in front of their noses wobbled open.

"Proceed towards the S-blocks," Mr Chor-Zor called out to them and the children walked forwards under the low roof. They could hear a hubbub of voices coming from somewhere out of sight and both guessed there were other tunnels nearby, full of students. Two flashing pink arrows appeared in the air at the end of the short corridor and the children walked towards them. The arrows vanished as soon they reached them. Charlie, of course, tried to run as fast as he could each time they appeared but never got near to one.

The next tunnel was narrow and lit by buzzing strip-lights hanging from the ceiling. There were thick, funnel cobwebs growing where the ceiling met the wall and puddles of smelly water on the floor which Charlie skipped around. More pink arrows appeared, flashing, in the furthest darkness, near a far-off corner. Again Charlie went for them, trying different tricks but again failed.

"Desist with the games," came a voice from behind them and both children were surprised to see Mr Chor-Zor again, in silhouette. "Follow the arrows. No more, no less."

"Yes, sir."

"Yes, sir."

As they walked on down the damp tunnel, the mod was so quiet behind them that once Alice turned and was surprised he was still there. She caught him *zeroed*: this was when a modified powered off while unobserved – its *aspect* blank but for the barest features: eye-sockets, the faintest shape of a nose, mouth and lips. As soon as Chor-Zor registered Alice looking, his *aspect* flashed back into place.

"Boy!" he cried later.

Charlie stopped. "Me, sir?"

"This is your area. ST-33."

Charlie looked at the earthen wall and saw nothing but roots and something like a maggot, crawling, slipping through the mud. "Where, sir?"

"At your feet."

Looking down, Charlie saw the grill he was standing on had placemarks. Small pink arrows, flashing, indicated where he

III

should stand.

"Correctly position yourself, if you will."

"Bye," Charlie said to Alice.

"Bye."

And, in a puff of steam, Charlie descended.

IV

Mrs Mallowan allowed the Consuls to open the door of the Eleusinian Room for her and wafted in as everyone inside rose to stand. "Thank you for coming. We'll try to keep this as brief as we can," she declared, marching across to the dais which she'd had set up in front of the hanging library. As requested, her chair had been decorated in gold. When she was sitting down, and after a brief glance at the attendees, she motioned for them all to sit.

Ms Row-Lin had begun to follow Mrs Mallowan until she'd noticed that only one seat had been placed on the stage. Now, as the others sat, Row-Lin paused, careful to not show her embarrassment, before tracking back to a place by the door. As she got there Chor-Zor arrived and they shared a subtle nod.

"Her Majesty didn't want to share the throne?" Chor-Zor whispered.

"Who does she think she is?"

The Eleusinian Room was full but not packed. This meeting had been announced only a few hours earlier and attendance was not compulsory. The Magistrate was the school's governing body, made up of all the staff and a variety of school prefects, such as the Consuls. The teachers were automatically members but the students had to be elected by majority votes. Members of the Magistrate had special privileges in the school. The Magistrate itself had a strange, legendary history, told in various books and objects dotted about the walls, but today the business was very straightforward and, with the weather worsening, there was no time to lose.

"We've asked you all to come to decide on our course of action regarding the great storm which is due to reach the school tonight," Mrs Mallowan began, standing, towering over them. Her audience was a collection of all the different types of student and teacher at the school, human and machine. Behind her the steel bars of the hanging library glittered like the stars no one had seen for years.

"The real storm will be at the meeting tomorrow," an anonymous voice called out.

"What? Who said that?" Mrs Mallowan's small blue eyes scanned the rows of seats but the culprit, whoever it was, escaped detection. There was murmuring and shuffling.

"That's enough, that's enough." Mrs Mallowan gestured for silence. "Your Headmistress says: *That's Enough!*" In a moment the room was silent. "We really must press on with the business in hand. The coming storm. Now there have been various reports as to the severity of this, and..."

At the back of the hall, Chor-Zor leaned in towards Row-Lin. "Are you all right? You don't seem your usual self?"

"No, no, it's nothing."

A latecomer arrived and Chor-Zor took the opportunity to pull Row-Lin outside the door they'd opened. A moment later the two mods were alone in the corridor, the Eleusinian Room door closed behind them. "You can't see yourself," Chor-Zor told Row-Lin. "You should see your face. It's a picture."

"Huh. Of what?"

"Confusion."

"Not a picture then. A mirror."

"You're not happy about what's going on either, I see," Chor-Zor told her. "Not enjoying playing courtesan to our new queen?" He made a bleep which passed for a laugh.

"Ah, you know I don't think any of us are better than anyone else," Row-Lin replied. Her dark scarlet face was clouded, the features dimmed. She had been brought to the school by Mrs Mallowan, had lived and learned with her over years at St Francis'. "We're all equals under the sun, all companions. None of us are better than others, not in the final reckoning." Row-Lin's *aspect* was a picture of honest confusion.

"Which is why we can't bow and scape to her." Chor-Zor placed a hand on Row-Lin's shoulder. "I don't know who she thinks she is, up on her golden throne, but I remember her when she suffered a stroke and was bedridden, not that long ago. When was it? Three or four years ago?"

"Three." Row-Lin nodded.

"Three. Exactly. It was you, me and Mr Pull-Mun who managed to nurse her to back to health that time, wasn't it? We saved her life! And now she thinks she can lord it over us like she's somehow better than everyone else! If anything, she's the most frail being in the whole school!"

"It isn't right," Row-Lin replied, shaking her head. "Not right at all."

"Something should be done." Chor-Zor waited for Row-Lin to look up at him again. "Before she destroys everything the school stands for."

The doors opened behind them and Mrs Mallowan appeared. A great shuffling of chairs rumbled from inside the room. "Ah, here you two are. Conspiring!"

"There was a small emergency, Ma'am," Chor-Zor explained. "Fixed now."

"Well the vote is to keep the school open during the storm but for everyone to be safely inside, out of harm's way, an hour after supper."

Chor-Zor nodded. "That sounds very reasonable."

"We alone will patrol and command the main building. Ms Row-Lin, you will take the dome and, Mr Chor-Zor, you will make sure the tunnels are evacuated."

"Very well."

"Yes, Ma'am."

"Good night then," Mrs Mallowan told them, walking away towards the hall.

Chor-Zor caught Row-Lin's eye before they were engulfed in the flowing stream of bodies, flesh and metal, which came

IV

pouring out of the Eleusinian Room. He was pleased to have seen, from her *aspect*, that his words had not been in vain.

V

"Good morning." The doctor leant forwards in his chair and waggled his fingers at Alice. "Come in, come in, please. Don't be afraid."

The doctor was an odd mixture of human and machine. He'd obviously been modified – his eyes were whirring sockets and there was a bleeping memory extension covering one side of his head – but his skin was very human, wrinkled and liver-spotted, and he was dressed in the same old-fashioned style clothes Aunty Athy had been wearing.

"Have a seat, please. Right there. This shouldn't take a moment."

They were in a sealed white space, alone, although Alice quickly realised there must be people observing somewhere: the doctor was speaking quietly into a mouthpiece and sometimes tapping on a small screen he had lying at an angle beside him. Alice couldn't help noticing that his typing was careless and that many words were misspelt.

"Your name, please?" He shone a light into Alice's eyes and asked her to lean back in the chair.

"Alice. Alice Vonnegut."

"Date of birth?"

"I was born here," Alice replied. "But I'm not sure when. They use a different system when you're up there."

"On Mars, you mean?"

"Well, we were never actually on Mars. Well, once, but just for a few hours. Most of the time we were on the big space station they have orbiting Mars. That's where we lived. Where our school was. My parents both worked there."

The doctor was examining Alice's nostrils. "But you were born *here*, you say?"

"I was. Not far from the school, actually. My brother was

born in the New Lunar Colonies. We left Earth when I was about two."

"Your mother was a pupil here at St Francis', wasn't she?"

"Yes."

"Related to our own Ma'am Athy?"

"Ma'am Athy is our great-aunt."

"That's why your parents sent you here, I suppose?"

"Yes, I suppose. Ow!"

"I'm sorry." Whatever the doctor had tweaked from Alice's nostril, he now placed on the screen in front of him. "You look fine but protocol dictates we check everything. All tags must be removed. This must have been one from your school, perhaps for the library?" As the analysis began, the doctor's eyes telescoped in and out and he smiled like a shark. "Terrible storms you've been having up there on Mars, we've heard?"

"Yes."

"I'm very sorry. I hope your family are out of danger."

"I hope so too," replied Alice. Her eyes were watering from the removal of the tag. Contrary to what the doctor thought, the tag had in fact been an olfactory booster, to enhance her sense of smell during a Feelie she'd experienced on the space station. Alice had forgotten it was even there.

The transparent screen between them blinged and the doctor clapped his hands. "You're all set. You may go on through the door there and meet your new dorm-mates. You'll be expected to stay here for the next twenty-four hours – protocol, I'm afraid – but soon enough you'll be assimilated into the school."

Alice didn't know what to say. "Thanks. I think."

VI

Charlie finished his medical inspection and walked through the wall to find himself in another white room filled from floor to ceiling with hexagonal panels. A young girl about Charlie's age turned to him as he entered. She was folding clothes into a drawer which had come sliding out of one of the panels. Charlie quickly realised that behind and inside each panel was a sleeping-pod, just as there were on cruisers.

"Oh, sorry," he said, hands up. "I'm looking for the boy's dorm."

The girl had dark eyes and a snub nose. Her hair was combed up into a high ponytail and she was wearing a green tracksuit and white trainers. "Ha. Sorry, pal. There's no boys and girls anythings in Quarantine. They organise us by ages here. You're stuck with me, I'm afraid."

"Oh." As Charlie thought about what to say a drawer hissed out beside his left leg.

"That's yours."

Charlie leaned down and pressed his fists into the white mattress inside the drawer. "It's all right," he reported. "Soft but not too soft. Even smells OK."

The girl shot out a hand. Her hair was not neat: several long, wispy strands covered her face. "I'm Aurora."

"Charlie."

Aurora pointed at his eyebrows. "You're from Mars, right?"

"Sort of. My mum's still there. I was born in the NLCs." Charlie said this with a sniff, almost showing off. He turned his head away as he spoke: he was insecure about his lack of eyebrows. "Everyone else in the family is from Earth."

"Me too," came the reply and Aurora turned back to her clothes. There were small, slim pockets for clothes between the mattress and the sides of the drawers.

"'You too' what?"

"I'm from the NLCs."

Charlie forgot his worries and turned to face her. "No way! Where?"

"Jjohn's City."

"Ha! Me too!" Charlie sat on his bed. "This place reminds me a bit of that. When we used to go on school trips to the dark side we used to stay in pods like this."

"The rest of the school is not as bad as this," Aurora said. She rolled her eyes at the panelled walls and soft purple roof lights.

"You're not new here then?"

"Me? No! I've been here since I was born, I think. At least, it feels like that sometimes."

"But why are you in here?"

"My father." Aurora turned to the clothes. "Nothing, he's ill. Still lives in the NLCs, near Jjohn's City. I wanted to, you, you know, go back up there. Say goodbye. I got as far as Mid-Station but they wouldn't let me go any further. The quota of Earth immigrants had been met. There was a huge queue, a wait. I don't know. My visa wasn't for more than a week. It's complicated."

"Oh." Charlie wanted to say sorry but he couldn't. He watched the girl out of the corner of his eye and hoped she wasn't going to start crying. "What's this school like, then?"

"This place?" Aurora turned to look at him but quickly turned away again. Her eyes were red. "It used to be quite nice but right now it's terrible."

"Why?"

"Oh, because of the fighting. The mods. Mrs Mallowan. It's horrible."

"We met a mod before. Chor-something."

"Chor-Zor." Aurora narrowed her eyes, wrinkled her nose like a rabbit and shook her head. She seemed to be saying, *Don't talk about that. Not here. Not now.*

"We met Mrs Mallowan too. She's the Headmistress, right?"

"At the moment, but that's the whole problem. It's been bad for a while. Mrs Mallowan took over and tried to settle everything down but she's acting like she's a queen or something, annoying everyone, especially the mods. It's all coming to a head, anyway. There's a Magistrate's meeting tomorrow to sort it all out and everyone's nervous about it."

"Why don't they just have separate schools like they do on the Moon? One for humans, one for mods?"

"Ha! That would be too sensible." Aurora looked at Charlie and rolled her eyes. She walked over to him and stood very close, whispering in his ear, which tickled him: "It's not really about them. It's about the school. Controlling the school. The future of the school."

"Why?" Charlie's face was very close to hers.

"There are things here. History. It's a powerful place."

"And it can't be that bad if you're still here," whispered Charlie.

"Ha! Like I have a choice."

Aurora went back to folding her clothes. There was too much to say: too painful. If she had any choice in the matter she'd be with her father, taking care of him, but there was no escape for her. She was trapped. When she looked across at Charlie, she saw him lying on his white bunk with one hand behind his head.

"I can't believe boarding schools even exist down here anymore," Charlie said, staring up at the ceiling. "We joke about them. Everyone jokes about them. Why does anyone have to be gathered in one place anymore? It's so weird."

"The dome, maybe? Doing experiments and things."

"Yeah, but you can do that virtually these days too. No one would think of going, *physically*, to *an actual school* on the Fourth or in the NLCs. I had some friends I used to do lessons with who'd never even met a real person. They liked it, said it was healthier."

"What's it like on the Fourth?" Aurora asked. The Fourth was another name people used for Mars.

"It's *guai*." Charlie used a Martian slang word, which he translated for Aurora: *guai* meant *good*. "The coolest thing are the Feelies. They're like a total, complete immersion experience. Like, you go into the whole thing, sight and mind. I've done quite a few but I have got friends who've cruised the Event Horizon and surfed Wormholes – that's another level." He stopped, remembering where he was. "I feel like I'm in one now, actually." Charlie shook his head. "A really bad one."

"I like the NLCs but my parents sent me down here for the fresh air. Huh. So ironic."

"Yeah, what's all that about?" Charlie asked. "The brown sky? It's horrible!"

"Pollution," replied Aurora, as if it was the most normal thing in the world. "The plastic won't degrade, people were greedy, nobody wanted to take care of anything. They ruined the weather, no one cared, so everyone suffers! Great!"

Charlie swore in Martian. "One of the reasons I wanted to come here was to play outside. I've never done it. I mean, I don't care that much. I've done loads of cool stuff. But it sounded fun. My mum and dad showed me loads of pictures. I swear the sky was blue in the stuff they showed me!"

"When I first came here we could play outside most days." Aurora closed her eyes. "I don't think the sky was ever blue, though. A bit green, maybe. Yellow mostly."

"Wow, what was that like? Playing outside?"

"Weird! So strange to have, like, no roof." Aurora looked happy. "You look up and," she stopped and bit her finger. "I can't remember if there were birds then."

"Spaceships?"

"No. Birds, *birds*." Aurora put her hands together and made two wings. "Fluttering about."

Charlie was lost for words.

"One minute!" came a booming voice.

"One minute?" asked Charlie.

"To lights out." Aurora giggled. As she took off her shoes she turned to Charlie. "Remember you activate the panel with your palm, OK? Put your hand straight up when you get locked in and you'll feel the mould."

"Straight up? All right. Thanks. What do we have in there?"

"Don't get excited. A food pill, I think. Hydration tubes."

"Nothing to watch?"

"They mix the air. You'll be asleep before you know it."

"Thirty seconds!"

"Thanks," Charlie said. He lay down, waggled about and giggled.

Aurora was laughing. She crossed her hands on her chest as protocol dictated. "Good night!"

"Ten seconds!"

"Night! Nice to meet you!"

"Five! Drawers closing!"

"And you!"

"Sealing. Sealing."

"Night!"

VII

Mr Chor-Zor stood at the crossroads swishing a red spotlight back and forth down the long, empty tunnels. Lightning exploded in juddering flashes, the jagged white bolts arrowing to Earth as from the fingertips of angry gods.

Chor-Zor was on the lookout for anyone breaking the curfew, searching for warm cyborg circuits as well as human hearts: no one must be left out.

The longest tunnel at St Francis', known as The Path, connected the main building with the dome and the vast subterranean hangars under what had once been the school playing fields. Chor-Zor stood at a crossing point known as The Steps. On a whim he turned northwards, striding up the long, snaking tunnel called The Road which led to The Kwad, the main teaching area.

Although at first this earthen, dank passageway seemed as deserted as all the others, Chor-Zor's instruments detected something unusual further ahead, near a security seal which led to the outside: the village exit. Weather interference meant it was difficult to pin down exactly what he was going to find but the readings indicated a life-form. Chor-Zor picked up the pace.

Dirty rain pelted the tunnel roof and the Moon, when the clouds parted, stared down like an angry, lidless eye. As the corridor lighting flickered and failed Chor-Zor switched to night vision but this too was affected by the storm which was now directly overhead.

There came a moment – fiery lightning legs scorching the tunnel roof itself – when the teacher lost all systems and threw the stick to one side. Thunder shook the walls and buckled the curved panels but Chor-Zor was undeterred. A growing conviction that the storm was a sign that things were not right at the school, that this was a time of great change, was developing in his mind. As night removed day, he thought, so this storm

29

was a sign that the old ways must change; that someone should be removed.

A flash lit up a shape crouched in the centre of the tunnel ahead and for one terrible moment Chor-Zor thought it was a wild, mythical animal – a lion, perhaps – for it had the same form. Fear turned to shame as he realised the figure was Pull-Mun, a fellow modified teacher, and immediately he made the secret salute the mods used among themselves when they were alone. "To perfection!"

"To perfection!" replied the other teacher. He was carrying a wet, black satchel.

"What are you doing all the way out here? And why are you soaking wet?"

"I've been outside." Pull-Mun's cape was plastered to his back with rain. He was broader than Chor-Zor, physically stronger though less intelligent. His *aspect* was apologetic: thick eyebrows and a mouth that was always slightly open. His designer had modelled him on an old human teacher he'd liked, wise and benign, but Pull-Mun's capabilities were far more basic and it showed.

"Outside? In *this*? Are you insane?"

"What a night this is! Such strange things!" Pull-Mun looked up at the rain streaming down the ceiling panels. "I swear I saw creatures out there, moving about. The storm had churned up the earth. I saw lightning hit dead bodies which had been washed up from the graves. The electricity brought them back to life! Haven't you heard about things like that? In the old stories? The old legends?"

Chor-Zor put both hands on the other teacher's shoulders. "I agree with you that this storm means something. All this weather, so strange. It is a sign that things are not right. It is a sign that things have to change."

"Ah! So you too have heard?"

"Heard what?"

"About what she's going to do tomorrow?" Dirty rainwater streaked Pull-Mun's slick, dark head.

"What do you mean? Who?"

"At the Magistrate meeting tomorrow," Pull-Mun began, smiling in a strange, menacing manner, "she is going to declare herself Headmistress for life."

"What?" Chor-Zor stepped away from the other man, shocked at the news. "But that's... that's impossible. It's against all the rules. How do you know this?"

"I know." Pull-Man held up his hand and a small orb of pink energy glowed and pulsed in the palm. "We all know this."

"Who is this 'all'?"

"Look. Read. Listen. Learn." Stepping forwards, Pull-Mun transferred the pulsing information to Chor-Zor's receptors. "Testimonies. Against her. Almost all from mods, it's true, but many, too, from humans." Pull-Man showed his teeth, hissing: "Everyone's had enough of her highness."

Chor-Zor assimilated the information. Pull-Mun was right. It sounded as though almost all the teachers were against Mrs Mallowan. "Why wasn't I told about this?"

"We couldn't tell you."

"Why not?"

"Because of your relationship with Ms Row-Lin. You are very close to her and she, in turn, is very close to Mrs Mallowan." Pull-Mun looked up at the mad storm. "All this chaos! Madness! The world is with us. Against her!"

"Oh, me too! I, too, am with you." Chor-Zor put his arm around his colleague's shoulders. He was shocked and relieved by the turn of events. "Well, for what it's worth I've been thinking about all this for some time, as we all have, of course, as we all have. And it might interest you to know that Ms Row-Lin has been thinking about it, too. And you're right – all of you. It should be done. *It must be done.* But we need Row-Lin. We need Row-Lin with us. Only if we all act together can this work."

"She's Mallowan's closest ally. She'd never agree to do anything to hurt her."

"Don't be so sure, my friend." Chor-Zor lifted his glove, showing Pull-Mun the pink orb of testimonies. "When she knows the depth of feeling against Mrs Mallowan, I'm quite sure she will join us and we can solve this issue once and for all." He remembered the conversation he'd had with Row-Lin outside the Eleusinian Room earlier that day. "In fact, I'm quite sure she is ready to join us."

"But that's fantastic news! If she joins us, there'll be no stopping us."

"For the good of the school the deed must happen," Chor-Zor said, his eyes as bright as the flashing lightning. "It's a logical conclusion our colleagues have come to. It's a logical step *we* must take. What Mrs Mallowan is doing is trying to cling on to power because *she* wants power, not because it's best for the school or any of us, humans or modifieds. It's nonsense!"

Pull-Mun, always easy to convince, was nodding. "I also believe we must think of the school, sir. That's what we all think! No one should be king or queen, a tyrant lording it above everyone else. We *all* need to all be in control of such an important thing as a school."

Chor-Zor pointed at the lightning, hand again on Pull-Mun's shoulder. "You were right to think that this storm was a sign, my friend. It is indeed a sign. This storm is a call to arms. The very Earth is begging us to do what is right – to take back control!"

Pull-Mun nodded. "I am so pleased you agree with us!" He turned in a circle. "It seems there might be an end to all this, after all."

"I tell you, sir, all this is natural. It's natural we all think alike. Never forget that we are nature's slaves, my friend. We are visitors here, part of nature. Although we think we are in control, although we sometimes think – as Ma'am Mallowan does – that we are above nature, above the rules of the universe – a deeper understanding reveals that we are just a small part of the grand organism, that great thing which is life. Nature created us and nature will destroy us, that is true. But we will not destroy ourselves and we will not allow anyone else to destroy us!"

Pull-Mun clasped his dripping hands together. "I'm so glad I came back!"

"We must take courage from the storm, my friend! Take courage from our mission!"

They walked back down the long, flashing tunnel together, shoulder to dark shoulder. In the wet, black satchel at Pull-Mun's side clattered a bag of laser knives.

VIII

Mrs Mallowan sat bolt upright in bed.

She'd heard something: had someone broken into the flat? Even though she'd closed the protective shutters, she could hear the storm roaring outside and judging from the thrusts and billows it was worse than she'd thought it would be. What time was it? Late. The middle of the night. Now she heard a scream and thought: *Roald!*

When she made it to her grandson's room her hands shot up to her face: his bed was ruffled but empty. The window had been blown open and the broken shutters were flapping on their hinges, the torn curtains billowing inwards. The Moon stared back at her as raindrops streamed in like white rats. Leaves and dirty, foul, stinking air barged in and around the walls and Mrs Mallowan's first reaction was to close the window but first, terrified Roald might be outside, she ran across and screamed the boy's name into the storm.

"I'm here, Nan," came a voice from behind her.

Mrs Mallowan turned, thin face icy-cold with rain, and saw the boy crumpled up behind the door, his knees drawn up to his chin. He was all skin and bones, like her, and his high forehead shone silver. Mrs Mallowan locked the window and knelt by him in her nightgown. "What happened, Roald? What happened, my dear?"

"Terrible nightmare." Roald was shaking. His teeth chattered.

"Oh, no! Again?"

The boy touched his grandmother's face. "You're alive! Are you really alive?"

Over the noise of the storm, both heard a knocking on the door. Mrs Mallowan touched her hand against her grandson's forehead. "You're ill, Roald."

"They killed you... downstairs. The mods. In the meeting

room – the Eleusinian Room!"

"We haven't had the meeting yet, Roald. It's tomorrow! You've had a bad dream again, that's all. You really are *very* highly strung."

The knocking came again.

"Don't answer it, Nan!" Roald backed up against the wall.

"Don't be silly, Roald! I'm the Headmistress." Mrs Mallowan stood. "If people can't come to me when they have a problem, who can they come to?"

"It was so real," muttered the boy. He held his shaking hands up in front of his face as if trying to convince himself he was really awake. There had been blood on his hands in the dream: he had been one of them, crowding in on her, raising a knife.

Peering through the fisheye, the Headmistress saw Mrs Jull-Costa, wide-eyed with rollers in her hair. Mrs Mallowan placed her palm flat on the wall reader, the door unlocked and Athy stepped inside, apologising. She looked even more shook up than Roald. "You can't go to that meeting tomorrow, Agatha," she gasped, looking back, half-terrified, down the empty corridor.

"What on earth's got into you now?"

"I had a terrible dream. A terrible, terrible dream." Athy stopped dead when she saw young Roald crumpled up at the foot of the wall. "Oh, my dear boy, what happened?"

"Another one afraid of storms," Mrs Mallowan hissed. "Now come along, both of you – into my study. I'll make us some strong tea and see if you can pull yourselves together."

The Headmistress stalked off as the wind tried to unhinge the windows. Athy helped Roald up and the two of them shuffled along, an odd couple, to Mrs Mallowan's small study. There was a small fire in the grate but the wind was so strong it blew down the chimney and made the flames dance low, howling with pleasure as it did so.

"Water, it'll have to be," Mrs Mallowan declared, holding up the cold kettle. "Nothing in here wants to work."

"I must talk to you in private, Agatha," Athy said, taking a step across the carpet towards the Headmistress. She meant she didn't want to speak in front of Roald. The boy was very pale, nestled deep among the cushions of his armchair, staring balefully at the tiny orange reeds flickering back and forth.

"Nonsense, Athy! I've had enough of all this. Draw up a seat and talk sense, woman, please. Whatever you have to say, you can say in front of him."

"It was the dream," Athy said, sitting down. "So very real. This has only happened to me once before in my life."

"A dream," repeated Mrs Mallowan with contempt.

"In the dream Romulus and Remus spoke to me."

"Your cats?" Folded arms, arched back, chin jutted.

"Yes." For the first time a look of doubt crossed Athy's own face. Sometimes dreams could seem so logical and real until you spoke them aloud. They had a logic which worked while they were yours and yours alone. The magic of a trick was destroyed when the secret was shared. "They said," Athy told Mrs Mallowan slowly, "that you should beware the Ides of March."

"The Ides of March? Oh, good lord." Mrs Mallowan looked up at the bare ceiling, exasperated. "What's this now? Shakespeare? Rome? *Antony and Cleopatra*, is it?"

"*Julius Caesar*, Nan," Roald corrected, quietly. "We've just finished reading it in Ancient Literature."

"Whose class was that?" asked Mrs Mallowan, squinting.

"Mine," replied Athy. She shrugged.

"Of course it was." The Headmistress put a curled white finger to her mouth. "The Ides of March. The Ides of March." She pressed a button on the table in front of her and a calendar sizzled silently into view. "When is it exactly? It refers to a date, does it not?"

"The fifteenth of March," Athy said.

"Tomorrow."

"Exactly." Athy was glad that she was being finally taken

seriously.

"And this Mr Shakespeare." Mrs Mallowan walked over to the heavy drapes covering the shuddering windows. "Legend says he was a teacher here, doesn't it?"

"Does it?" Roald sat forwards, colour in his cheeks for the first time.

"That's what I believe." Athy followed the Headmistress with her eyes and winked at Roald.

"That's your theory, is it?"

"There are certain parallels between the school's history and the plays..."

"Of the ancient playwright."

"Still widely read."

"In your underattended classes?"

"All over the world."

"Oh, come now, Athy. *Nobody* reads these days. And even less people see plays."

"Well that depends," Athy began.

"Now that I think about it, don't your magical, fortune-telling cats have strange names?"

"Romulus and Remus."

"Another of our Mr Shakespeare's plays?" asked Mrs Mallowan.

"The founders of Rome," replied Athy, slightly shocked at her colleague's ignorance.

"More legends and dreams," Mrs Mallowan said, wafting a hand. After an intake of breath and a pause, she turned to them and spoke in a clear, ringing voice: "Superstition is for those who believe they can change fate. It is for those who believe they can change what the world has in store for them. For both of your information, I am not one of those people." She walked across to the fire and stood stick thin in front of it, a narrow shadow.

"The way I see it, you are both afraid. Afraid for me, I can see that, and I can feel it. But what I can really sense is your *own* fear.

That *you* are afraid. You seem to think that something terrible is going to happen to me but let me tell you both something: I have no fear of death." She smiled. "I am not afraid. I am not afraid of life and death holds no mystery to me. I am ready for death. I accept it as a part of life. There is absolutely no reason for you to be afraid for me."

Roald sighed. "I wish we were all as brave as you, Nan."

"Always embrace the unexpected, Roald," Mrs Mallowan told him, bending slightly, pointing a finger. "Don't be afraid of it." She straightened up, lifting her hands. "Look fear right in the face. Bring it out into the open. Stare it down, don't let it hide in the shadows, in your mind, growling and growing and torturing you." She examined Athy and Roald with pity. "What do you think happens to everyone and everything in this life? That we live forever?"

"How do you explain that we've both had the same bad dreams, Nan?" Roald asked, but the fight was gone out of him. He was awake now and his nightmares and fears seemed silly.

"If it doesn't sound too conceited, I think it's because you both care very much for me and that you know the situation here at the school is very dangerous. But these dreams are only your worries talking. Your fears. But I am not worried and I am not afraid. If something terrible is going to happen tomorrow, it will happen, that's all there is to it."

Athy accepted this but asked, "Is there really no way you will reconsider going to that meeting tomorrow, Agatha?"

"Of course not. I'm going. I have to, I must, I want to and I will."

"Oh, Nan." Roald walked over to Mrs Mallowan and hugged her.

"Now if you don't mind, I think we should all go back to bed. I, for one, need my sleep."

"Yes, of course. Goodnight, Agatha," Athy said.

She let herself out and walked back down the rattling corridor, past the flashing windows, to the main staircase. But instead of going upstairs to her own flat, she went down the staircase and padded across the ground floor in her stockinged feet.

The stern, empty chimney in the main hall growled and boomed as she rushed by in the shadows and she only stopped when she got to the door of the Eleusinian Room. She was a member of the Magistrate – the school's prefect and governing body – and so gaining access was not a problem.

Once inside, the usual green light leaking from the stained-glass windows in the roof tower, Athy went directly to the small, curtained cubbyhole halfway up the wall near the school's famous hanging library. This cubbyhole was St Francis' holy of holies: in a moment she'd reached in and taken The Book, the school's oldest and most treasured possession. A second more and she was back outside, the door closed, slithering across the cold hall floor towards the staircase in her socks.

Perhaps Mrs Mallowan's enemies would be able to do what they wanted tomorrow. Athy was convinced something terrible *would* happen. But if Mrs Mallowan was determined to walk straight into their trap, *she* would do something. The conspirators could do what they wanted with each of the teachers but they – Athy decided – would have a fight on their hands when it came to stealing the spirit of the school.

She disappeared upstairs into the shadows with the The Book poking out from under the arm of her pink nightdress, lightning flashing on the pink rollers in her grey hair.

IX

Alice was woken by a soft, tinging bell, a sense of movement and a woman's voice saying quietly, gently: *Good morning, Alice. You have cleared quarantine and are free to go to school. Please put on the uniform provided and follow the pink signs to your first class. Follow protocol. Be perfect!*

The message repeated as Alice climbed out of her sleeping drawer and began to get dressed. The light was bright but more muted than she remembered from the night before. Soft music was tinkling from somewhere above the hissing, invisible ceiling.

Yawning, Alice pulled on a stretchy, green, all-in-one undergarment, and chose body-hugging trousers instead of an old-fashioned skirt. She wore a narrow-collared white shirt which buttoned itself and a dark green body warmer which she set to 'loose'.

Proceed to class, came the voice, as a dark doorway opened up in the wall of the room. *Proceed to class.*

In her field of vision Alice saw a pink arrow pointing towards the doorway and realised her eyes had been recalibrated as she slept. This was the third time she'd gone through the process in as many weeks – for the flight to the Moon, on the Moon itself and now here – and she felt the familiar itch when she blinked. But, she thought, these modifications were necessary. Without the eye adjustments you could easily get lost, and it was good to know how your body was in case you needed any medical treatment.

"Hi, I'm Roald," said a very pale, tired-looking boy who met her as she passed through the doorway. "I'm your Pair for the day. I'll take you and show you around. If you have any questions, just ask."

Alice smiled. "You sound really enthusiastic."

The boy grinned. His face was gaunt and serious, but when

he smiled he lit up. "Sorry, I'm just *so* tired. You know: the storm. Didn't sleep a wink."

"I didn't hear a thing," said Alice.

They shook hands and Alice stretched as Roald yawned so hard his eyes watered. It was good for Alice to be out of the cell, in a real environment. They were at a crossing point in the tunnels and she could see, through the clear, ribbed ceiling, the rising silver sphere of the dome. Uniformed children were milling along the busy corridor around them, chatting and shouting, more were filing in from both sides. The air outside looked pale yellow, clearer than it had been the day before, though a tinny voice was coming from hidden speakers warning the students to stay inside as further bad weather was expected mid-morning.

"So, where are we going first?" Alice asked.

"Class, I guess," Roald answered. "Stay close to me." He walked into the crowd in a daze, his head aching from lack of sleep, little fires burning behind his eyes. In truth he felt better now it was morning. He'd slept fitfully for a few hours right before dawn without any more worrying dreams but his soul was low.

They weaved in and out of pupils and teachers on the long corridor to the dome. "Is it really dangerous to go outside these days?" Alice asked because she was interested, but also because she wanted to try and communicate with the boy. Alice was a warm soul: her reaction to the boy's pain and loneliness was to try and soothe and cure it, not be repelled. He was such a funny-looking thing, like an old man in miniature, eyes crumpled and slightly bent like he had the weight of the world on his shoulders.

"Better to be safe than sorry," Roald replied, not really knowing what he meant. He was one of those people who'd always been told they were clever and so felt he had to give an answer to any question, even if he didn't know one. "Some people are immune to the viruses in the air but there's often no way of knowing until it's too late. There have been cases of people going outside and then infecting whole schools, domes and even cities."

"And are there really no animals anymore?" Alice looked up at the sad, empty sky. "No birds?"

"No birds, certainly. At least not in the wild. The plastic killed them in the end. Some insects have survived and adapted, as you know. We've heard stories of mutations, of huge caterpillars emerging from the Earth in the southern hemisphere. But there's nothing here." He seemed to think about this answer for a moment, and gave a little cough before adding, "Not animals, anyway."

Alice felt sad when she saw the state of the natural world. She had fond memories of her time on Earth: they had lived here for the first years of her life. They had pictures at home: Alice standing on beaches, squinting. Under green oaks, in fields. She remembered the smell of fresh air. Of cool, fresh air on summer mornings.

"Better than everything being red and rusty, though, eh?" Roald quipped. There was a hint of nastiness in his words, a hint of putting Alice in her place. You are a Martian so be careful of what you say about my planet.

Alice felt a familiar sinking feeling: wherever she had lived, she'd never quite fitted in. On Mars she and Charlie had been Earthers and here it looked like they would be Martians. She looked like a Martian, with no eyebrows and facial hair, but there was no dust on Mars or the Space Stations and so no need for them. Soon everyone on Earth would lose their eyebrows and nose hair, too, now that they couldn't go outside.

"I just think it's nice to see the sky," Alice replied quietly. "Whether it's blue, red or yellow."

"You've got domes on the Fourth, right?"

"Oh, yes. And on the Moon."

In the New Lunar Colonies, the name for the settlements on the Moon, the domes had been enormous but opaque: the atmosphere was constantly bombarded by space dust and the wall panels had to be thick and protected. When she'd first gone there, they'd kept the domes clean but on the last visit she noticed they'd let them get covered over with sand and dust.

"I keep having dreams about blue skies," Roald said, almost absent-mindedly. He was talking honestly, as if she wasn't even there. "I don't know if they're daydreams or my future or somewhere I was when I was young. They're so vivid. Like places I've been to. Or that I'm going to."

Alice stopped in front of him. "Are there any places with blue skies anymore?"

"That's just it," said Roald, sadly. For the first time he looked right at Alice and their eyes met. Both were friendly. "Not in our solar system, anyway."

"You could work on a deep-space cruiser? Try to make it to another system?"

Roald checked to see if the girl was joking with him. Nobody human could ever hope to work on a deep-space cruiser: for now only mods were allowed. "It's my dream," he answered, in a quiet, weak voice. It was strange to tell the truth. His recurring dreams and his dream job were his two biggest secrets and he'd told this stranger both already. He must be exhausted! "But it's dumb. I don't know why I bother. It's impossible."

"It's good to have a dream," Alice said, smiling. "It keeps you going forwards."

"Even if it's an illusion?"

"You don't know if it is, though, do you?" Alice nodded, smiling. "My dad always says, 'Follow your nose! Keep moving forwards!' It's the only way." To her surprise, Alice choked up. Talking about her father, using his words, made her miss him very sharply.

"Come through please, come through," instructed the green robot assistant manning the security gate outside the dome. The machine had a human-looking head but was incorporated into the gate itself, attached to the tunnel floor. "Keep moving forwards."

"See?" Alice said, swallowing the tears, smiling. "Even he agrees."

Roald laughed.

As they passed through the safety zone, the enormity of the dome opened up before them. "Wow," was Alice's honest response to the sight.

The air was incredibly sweet and Alice felt her eyes and lungs bulge as she took a breath. Trees and vines sprouted around and over the walls while running water trickled and splashed from fountains. The centre of the structure was divided into floors busy with students and teachers, half-visible in classrooms demarcated by fizzing smart-walls. Some of these classrooms were black, as though in shadow, but Alice knew from her schools on the Moon and Stations that the walls had been inverted and that interactive classes were taking place within, invisible from the floor.

"What did you study on the Fourth?" Roald asked.

"Mostly Inner," Alice replied. Studies were divided into I, IB and O: I, or Inner, was the study of everything smaller than an atom; O, or Outer, was the study of everything larger than a galaxy, and IB was all In-Between. Each division was then subdivided into specialisations.

"Your specialism?"

"The brain."

"Really? Mine too!" Roald grinned but then slapped his high forehead. "Actually, of course it is! That's why they put us together." He pointed up at a classroom high above the palm tree they were walking past. "We've got class with Mr Banks today. I think you'll like it."

Alice followed Roald as he navigated the busy ground floor, happy to see that most of the students smiled at her as they passed. All human types were here and all looked to be working together peacefully. Alice saw Martians and Lunarians, a few partials, some modifieds and even a smattering of uniformed cyborgs. The teachers were not so mixed: most seemed to be Earthlings and she didn't see any modifieds.

They took flying steps at a hub (normal for both Roald and Alice) which flew them swiftly up to the classroom Roald had pointed out. Alice waited patiently outside as Roald went in. She could feel the class examining her through the invisible walls and sometimes saw the teacher, who was tall, thin, bearded and had surgically-enhanced eyes which whizzled in and out, observe her too. Finally he beckoned to Alice: "All right then, missy. In you come."

The classroom was much larger than it looked like from outside. Inside it was enormous, a roofless space in which students were working at desks and stations floating in the air or attached by light-lines to the walls. Alice had seen classrooms like this in some of the official edu-domes on the Moon but had never had the luck to be able to use one.

"This is Alice," Mr Banks announced and there was a murmur of welcome. "Well. Perhaps you can tell me what you were working on up on the Fourth, Ms Vonnegut? Anything interesting?"

"The usual things, sir."

"All right." Mr Banks' left eye whirred outwards. "You've studied Inner, I see? What was the last thing you worked on?"

"Actually, it was a project I really liked. We'd just started."

"Oh, yes?"

"You want me to tell you about it?" Alice swayed, embarrassed.

"Please!"

"Well, we wanted to see what it was like to follow an idea during the first part of its life." Alice giggled and reddened. "I know it's a bit silly."

"No, no. It sounds very interesting. Do go on."

"Well, the plan was to document the start of an idea, see how an idea was born in the brain, how it formed."

Mr Banks stroked his chin. "To map the *journey* of an idea? From its inception?"

"Not just map it, sir." Alice put her hands over her face and peeped through her fingers. "Oh, if I tell you the truth, sir, it's going to sound silly."

"Try me." Mr Banks' attitude towards Alice had changed. He was now looking at her, really looking at her, his eyes whirring silently in and out. There was something about the girl that was so honest and open it fascinated him. These days everyone at the school was guarded and careful, students and staff.

"Well, I wanted to see what it was like to actually *ride* an idea. To sit on it. To get on at the first neuron explosion, at the instant the idea was born, and just ride it around the brain. I wanted to see how an idea chose, if it does choose, how it develops, which pathways it follows. I wanted to know if we are in control of our ideas or if our ideas are in control of us."

Mr Banks laughed. "Ha! I like it! How far did you get?"

Alice's nose wrinkled. "We had some trials. Some tests. It's one thing to chase the trail of an idea backwards but quite another thing to chase it forwards. I was working with my friends, two friends, and we were going to see if we could start in different places and join together somewhere, in the same story, but we had to stop."

"Why?"

"Because Mum said we had to come here."

"Ah." Mr Banks tapped the end of his nose. "I understand." He blinked and his eyes shot back into their sockets. "Well, I think you'd probably work best with Roald. He's been looking for a partner – even though he doesn't know it. He's quite the specialist with the Nano-pods. I suppose that's what you were using?"

Alice gave a little chuckle of delight. "Oh, yes! You have Nano-pods?"

"Sure we do. Not state of the art by any means, but useable. Come on. Grab an AGB there."

"Where?" Alice looked behind herself.

"An Anti-Gravity Belt. Those things there, hanging on the bar." Alice did as she was told, picking up a well-worn blue harness and connecting it around her waist and threading it between her legs as Mr Banks showed her how.

"You didn't have these on the Fourth?"

"Not in my school," Alice said. She'd got so used to people talking to her as if she'd lived all her life on Mars that she let the comments fly. You couldn't keep saying, *Well, actually, I was only there a few days visiting Mum's work. We spent most of our time living on a huge space station which orbited the planet doing almost exactly the same things as children everywhere in the galaxy do.* You disappointed people if you did that.

"You know, I'm thinking," Mr Banks said, checking their pathway was clear. "Perhaps you could give us all a short presentation on life on the Fourth one day, if you wouldn't mind? It might do this lot some good to be reminded that there's something going on outside St Francis'?"

"Maybe, sir."

"Aye, well, no rush. No pressure." Mr Banks smiled. "Right? Are we set?" He pressed the pad in the centre of the belt and lifted slowly off the floor. "That's it, just feel it, ease it. Good. Now use your mind, frontal lobe. Good, that's it. Don't worry, it's not powerful. Good, that's it, just float. Ears popping? Yes, yes. Good. Come on up."

They floated off the school floor and up through the classroom space. Alice nodded as students broke off from their experiments to say hello and smile back at her. She realised she felt far less nervous about being on Earth and being at a new school than she had done on the flight down. She'd prepared herself for St Francis' being so awful that the reality was actually quite pleasant.

"Roald!"

"Me again," Alice smiled, landing on the slightly darker whiteness which was Roald's workspace floor.

Roald nodded. That nice smile appeared under his dark eyes again. "Hi."

"Keep your belt on today," Mr Banks told Alice. "Just in case of any mishaps."

Alice's attention had already wandered. Roald's desktop was a display of particles – lurid green and electric blue.

"Tell Alice what all this is, Roald," Mr Banks said. "And then, Alice, you tell him about your idea."

"Well," Roald started. He put back on his dark glasses and through the lenses Alice could see he had multiple screens and applications open. He spoke from under the rim and so had to tilt his head right back. "Well, this is quite boring, actually. It's a map of the surface of the brain where I think ideas are born – the place an idea first pops up in your mind. Each of these snaky lines here are the random thoughts you have which make up the idea – the stimulus. See here, where they intersect – that's where I think they pop up as a fully formed idea. It's part of the cerebral cortex but it happens just above, you see? In the low atmosphere. I call the liquid here the Thought Sea."

Alice took the glasses she was offered and stared into the pretty galaxy of colours. "Wow. You picked the same place we did!"

"The same place?" Roald took off his glasses. He looked shocked. "What do you mean 'we did'?"

Mr Banks floated back down to the classroom floor.

X

Mrs Jull-Costa sat on her sofa with Romulus and Remus winding in and out of her ankles. The locket in her palm was warm, it had been rubbed so much.

She looked down at her hands, at the wrinkles and joints swollen with arthritis, and attached the locket to the chain she'd worn around her wrist ever since Kizzie had left the school. You needed both the brooch and the chain for the magic to work, Kizzie had said. Then, smiling to herself, Athy clipped open the locket and looked down at the sepia-coloured portrait of the *Mona Lisa* inside. "Hello again."

Her cats looked up and purred.

Had it ever really happened? All those years ago, the first time she'd ever tried it?

You look back into the past and think you remember things but sometimes your mind plays tricks on you. You make the past better than it really was. Summers were brighter. You were innocent in the past. It was softer, better. You cannot be hurt in the past as you can in the present and future.

Athy told herself, *Yes, it really happened. It really did.*

In her mind's eye she saw it all again. She saw herself lying in bed one night in the dorm, rain pelting on the window just like it was that morning. That night, as quietly as she could, she'd whispered the words Kizzie had written inside the brooch and she'd lain there, eyes wide open, staring up at the hissing darkness, listening to the downpour.

She forgot the mewling cats and the rumbling storm. She forgot how old she was, her bad dreams and the pain in her hips. She even forgot the Magistrate's meeting.

She'd found herself at the end of a dark corridor. It had happened in a blink.

In the distance she saw daylight and a lady with long, dark

hair sitting on a chair. The lady was sideways on to Athy, looking straight ahead, nodding towards a man whose deep voice she could hear talking, bossing people about.

The light the lady was sitting in was coming from an open window directly behind her shoulders, out of sight. Athy, hiding in some kind of dark passageway, heard the noise of a street: dogs yapping, birdsong, the steady rumble of wooden wheels on cobbles and clattering hooves. The pale curtain was fluttering and the seated woman was chatting to people Athy couldn't see.

The woman turned to one side and Athy recognised her. How odd to see her alive, a real, breathing woman, sitting there, on a chair, right in front of her. *Is that really her?* she thought. *How can I be in the picture?*

Scared, Athy pulled up the heavy, dark drapes beside her and ducked underneath. The wall behind was cold stone and when she stood upright she found a square window of dark, thick, green glass. Athy could just about make out market stalls set up around a sprinkling fountain in a square below. The window was like looking through the bottom of a bottle. Horses and carts passed by and a seller was handing out orange quarters.

Ducking back under the drapes, which smelled like church, Athy edged up the corridor. Two people, a man and a woman, carried what looked like a rolled-up carpet past the sitting woman and stood on chairs behind her, unravelling the roll from ceiling to floor and covering the window, blocking most of the light. The man, dressed, like everyone Athy could see, in old-fashioned clothes, shouted: "What do you want me to do with this, maestro? Nail it into place?"

"Nail it, yes! Nail it, nail it!"

The sitter yawned, turning her head as she did so, and this time she caught sight of Athy. Immediately the lady widened her eyes. Athy stood rooted to the spot, not sure whether to stay or run but the woman winked and, in an instant, Athy knew she was safe.

Out of sight, the boss was shouting orders. He had the voice of a giant.

"I'll stretch my legs while you nail that up," the lady said to the out-of-sight man, standing, hitching up her bustling black dresses and coming down into the corridor to kneel in front of Athy. She had a smiling, cat-like face and neat teeth. "And who might you be, little girl?" She touched Athy's cheek with a soft finger.

"I came from," Athy looked behind herself but there was nothing. A blank wall of black drapes. "Actually, I don't know."

The lady threw her hair over one shoulder and laughed. "How long have you been hiding in here?" She smelled so fresh and flowery it made Athy feel sleepy.

"Not long." Athy was so confused by everything that the odd tone of her own voice – the strange words coming out of her mouth – hardly bothered her. She found herself enjoying looking into the woman's eyes. The lady had kindly eyes, shaped like almonds.

"Are you playing with Pierro? Is that what you're up to?"

Athy nodded, seeing a way out: an explanation. "Hide and seek," she added, reddening at the lie.

The lady touched her face again. "Well, you shouldn't hide here, little thing, he'll find you too easily. Pierro knows this place." The lady giggled, thinking something to herself. "I have an idea." She knelt closer and cupped her hand to Athy's ear. "Listen. Why don't you…"

"Donna Lisa!" A tall, bearded man with wild, greying hair appeared beside the empty chair at the end of the corridor. He was the owner of the deep, loud voice Athy had been hearing: obviously the boss, the *maestro*. He was standing with his hands on his hips, barefoot. "Where are you? Are you down there?"

"Yes, I'm here. Coming now!"

"What the devil are you doing? Come on, please, Lisa, we really *must* get on."

The lady stood up – she was still sore after the birth of Andrea – and took a moment to arrange her skirts. "Have they finished arranging the screen? I can't be getting showered with dust again."

"It's taken care of," nodded the painter as Lisa came slowly back to the main room and the light. The *maestro* wore a smock covered with smudges and streaks of paint. His hands, especially his nails, were black. "What on earth were you doing in there? Are you all right? You not feeling well or something?"

"No, no, I'm fine. I was trying to see where Francesco put the missing trunk." Lisa tapped the painter's hand and retook her seat. "Thanks, Leo. I'm fine now. Let's continue. Please." She turned to look at the hanging sheet, a painted landscape. "Oh, I like that."

"My world," winked the painter. He knelt in front of her, a brush clamped between his teeth, strands of grey hair like frayed knots dangling in front of his big nose, and arranged Lisa's hands. "Keep very still."

"This chair is most uncomfortable."

"Move a little to the side, please, my dear. To *my* side, my side, not your side."

Leo the painter made Lisa shuffle back and forth until he was happy with where she was sitting in relation to the screen nailed to the wall behind her. The backdrop was important to Leonardo, a vision of the countryside where he had been born, and he'd spent more time on getting it right than he would on Lisa's portrait. Painting Lisa was business. Painting home was pleasure.

"Right then," he declared, finally happy. He turned to face his three students and their easels, all set up in front of the bright windows on the other side of the room beyond which lay the towers and roofs of Florence. "No lines, as I said. Nature does not contain lines. There are no such things as lines and borders. We shall work until you achieve the effect I showed you before.

Patience. Only patience begets good work."

At that moment Athy, concealed under Lisa's skirts, sneezed.

Leo and the other painters looked across in surprise and Lisa giggled. "I apologise."

"Bless you," an assistant, sitting on a stool, said. He held up his brush to help with perspective.

"There's something going on," the female student whispered. "Under her... you know..."

"Silence!" hissed Leo. "Paint!"

Well aware that his subject was up to something, the *maestro* nevertheless liked the smile which had formed on Lisa's lips and snatched at his paint-board, eager to catch the effect. His students did as they were told but a second sneeze blew Athy's cover and one of the male assistants raced across to hitch up Lisa's skirts. "There's a little girl under here!" he shouted, as if he'd won something.

"She's only playing hide and seek!" Lisa replied, laughing.

Athy darted out and began to run back and forth across the studio, evading the grasping hands trying to capture her. All the while Lisa watched, rocking backwards slightly, clapping with pleasure, and Leo, at his easel, caught each movement of her eyes, each birdlike twitch, and, in his own world, in his own silence, quickly recorded these observations on his canvas. It was only when Athy, running for the corridor, knocked over a large vase, that he exploded, crying: "*Haaaaaalt!*"

Athy had never been shouted at so loudly before in her life and she froze immediately, her ears ringing.

For a moment there was no noise, only birdsong and street murmurs, but then Athy saw all the painters pointing at her and looked down and found, with shock, that where she was wet with spilt water from the brush pots, she had gone transparent. She could see the floorboards through her own arm, see the carpet through her waist.

"A devil!" a woman hissed, crossing herself.

"Witchcraft!"

Athy, half-terrified, ran back down the shadowy corridor and yanked open the little green window behind the drapes. She scrambled up and surprised a pigeon on the roof. Looking down, she saw she was above the fountain. Its circle of blue was wide and looked deep enough to take her if she jumped. *I must bend my knees*, she told herself. *Or I'll break my legs.*

Lisa arrived and called out to her to get down from the ledge but Athy leapt off and landed in the cold water of the fountain, disappearing immediately. Two old men sitting nearby stood up and prodded the water with their walking sticks, gobsmacked.

Athy opened her eyes and gasped. She saw the ceiling of the dorm. The old, peeling panels on the ceiling. Cobwebs and dust. Kizzie's face appeared from the top bunk. "Welcome back. Did you have a nice trip?"

"It worked," Athy gasped.

Kizzie reached out and touched her sister's hand. "Enjoy it?"

"It was so real," was all Athy could say, breathless. She sat up. The other girls were asleep. Her nightdress and hair were wet, the bed too. "I jumped into a fountain."

"Water is the only thing that will bring you back," Kizzie said, slipping down to the floor. "Come on, we need to change the bed."

Athy sat up. "Can I really do that again?"

"Twice more, while there's a full Moon," Kizzie said. She looked sharply at her sister. "Did you bring the brooch and chain back?"

"Yes, here."

"Good." Kizzie smiled. "Don't ever drop it or leave it or you'll never get back."

Athy stood up and changed, looking out through the cold black panes at the full Moon beaming in at her, so bright it blocked out all the stars.

"You see?" Kizzie said, balling up the sheets. "There's more to this world than you can ever dream of, Athy. The key to it all is to never stop dreaming!"

XI

Charlie glanced up at Aurora. "What?" His eyes went back down to his interactive desk where he was watching sokker videos.

"You weren't listening, were you?" Aurora sighed.

"To what?"

"To anything!"

Although Charlie continued to stare at the screen, Aurora couldn't help liking him. He was independent and strong-headed, different from the other boys in the class. He didn't seem to fear the teachers as much as the others but he didn't show off about it either – he genuinely didn't seem to care.

"You just asked me if I was listening," he said to her now, quickly making eye contact again. "See? I was listening."

They'd gone to breakfast together that morning. Aurora had been instructed to guide him through the day, to be his Pair. Now they were in Waking Knowledge in the Kwad, the main underground classroom area. The teacher, Mr Byron, had asked them to work together and they were supposed to be coming up with ideas for a new project.

"Oh, come on, Charlie. Look at me. Turn that off. You'll get us both into trouble if Byron catches you watching stuff like that, you know."

"So? What's he going to do? We slept in pods last night, remember?"

"There's *way* worse things they can do to you."

"Like what?"

"Like being kept in at the weekend with BLUE-OOM."

Charlie looked up and pulled a face. "That just sounds silly."

"Only because you don't know what it is."

"They've got you all scared here. You're like *anclas*." Anclas were Martian droids which people used for basic menial tasks in the home. They were programmed never to reject an order.

"We're supposed to be working in pairs, Charlie, and I've been put with you. Sorry if that interrupts your viewing of old sokker rubbish." Aurora nudged Charlie's arm. "Can't we just do what we have to do and then you can watch your stuff?"

Charlie began to sigh but suddenly noticed the teacher, Mr Byron, heading in their direction. Playing it very cool, he swished a hand over the screen to disilluminate it and, continuing the movement, ran his fingers through his fringe. In the most bored, put-upon voice he could muster, he put his chin on the white table and said: "Go on, then, oh great mistress. Tell me what we're supposed to do."

"Idiot." Aurora slid her stool beside Charlie's and combed a loose strand of hair behind one of her ears. "I did just tell you, you know."

They were in a small room which needed a lick of paint and lots of fresh air. The vents hummed in the walls but the breeze they pumped out smelled faintly of cabbage. There were cracks in the draught pipes, and the odours from the cesspits and drains running even deeper under the earth than the classrooms seeped up into the rooms. Patches of moss and lichen were starting to show through the painted walls, particularly in the corner behind Charlie and Aurora.

Charlie wagged his hand under his nose. "This place proper reeks."

"Old legends."

"What?" Charlie frowned. "Ah, that's what we're supposed to be doing. Right. Good. Old legends." He screwed up his face. "What does that even mean?"

"I suppose it means you don't know any."

"Ha, ha, ha." Charlie pulled the top of his green, all-in-one underwear up over his mouth like a mask. "I feel like I'm suffocating. I'm seriously going to vomit. Everyone in the solar system talks about Earth air and then you come here and it's like being stuck in a room with week-old farts. So ironic."

"No fresh air until two today, I'm afraid, Vonnegut," Mr Byron declared, appearing behind them, "but I shall up the ventilation level if you are as uncomfortable as you say."

"That would be amazing, sir."

Almost immediately a humming resounded from the vents at their feet and a fresh layer of dust shook off the ceiling. Warm, recycled air swirled like invisible eels around their ankles. Mr Byron sidled off.

"What are 'old legends' anyway?" Charlie asked, pointing at the illuminated words which were circling in the middle of the room. He leaned on his own arm and began to bite his fingernails. He'd bitten his nails since he was a child. If he was alone and sockless he ate the nails on his feet. Sometimes he chewed the sleeve of his clothes, or gloves if he had them on. He was like a rodent that had to eat or its teeth would continue to grow and eventually suffocate it. The irony was, despite all this nibbling, he was stick thin.

"Old wars, history, all that sort of thing."

"Puff. I don't know anything about that. Really."

"Didn't they teach you history on Mars?"

"Bits. They teach you Mars stuff there, though. Mars history."
I wasn't on Mars that long, he heard the good voice in his head tell him. *Oh, leave it*, replied the bad. *She likes it.*

"Yep, that's like us. All the classes in the NLCs were about the Moon. Do you know they're moving the graves of all the famous people from Earth to the Moon?"

"Really?"

"Yes. Because the soil down here is becoming too acidic. There's already lots of famous people up there. They can preserve them longer, apparently. Some people in my class said it's because they want to grow them again up there, like, clones. There's a company doing it. My dad always said that was impossible. At least, he hoped it was impossible because it sounds so creepy. And it is a bit creepy, isn't it?"

"I don't get why we have to learn history in the first place. If it's already happened what does it matter if you know it or not?"

"Agreed. But if we could choose what we did and didn't learn, school wouldn't be school, right?" Aurora stared into Charlie's eyes and winked. "Life is suffering, Charlie. Haven't you heard? They worked that out *ages* ago."

"Only because we have to go to school," Charlie replied. He liked Aurora's eyes. If you looked really closely at the black pupil in the centre it looked like a planet in eclipse. A sun, not our sun but another star, was right behind the planet, throwing off light flares. There could be a whole universe in there, in her eyes. He was about to tell her all this – at least the part about the pupil looking like a planet in eclipse – when he heard the teacher's voice.

"Five minutes," Mr Byron called out.

"Oh no," said Charlie, rolling his eyes and dropping his head to the blank screen. "We're dead!"

"Wait, I have an idea," Aurora began. "It's probably not good, but it's something."

"What? 'Life is suffering'?" Charlie kicked his boot heels into the bars on the stool he was sitting on.

"I was thinking that we could do something about the history of St Francis'. Maybe choose one of the places? Even the Kwad, maybe the Main Building?"

"For what?"

"To try and tell the story of what it was like in the past and what it's like now." Aurora drummed her smart-pen against her chin. "Like, we could picture it now and put things over it, to show people what it was like then."

"Make a feelie?" Charlie asked, finally showing interest. He straightened up.

"Yes, maybe. But – well, I'm not sure about that." Aurora was trying to think. She had her back very straight. "I don't really know what a 'feelie' is."

"Yeah but I do! They're great! I've done them before. I can do that bit. You choose it, the subject or whatever – but not the Kwad, not this place, this place stinks and is miserable – but you put in all the stuff you want to put, and I'll direct it."

"Really? I can choose what I want it to be about? You don't care?"

"Yeah, yeah, whatever." Charlie nodded, leaning back on his stool with his hands crossed behind his head. "You choose the place, you find what it was like and get all the photos or films whatever, and I'll turn it into a feelie. It'll be *jakk*! People will be able to, like, *feel* what it was like to be there in the past. That would be *jakkik*, really."

"It's not exactly what we're supposed to do," Aurora said, worried.

"But it's fine," replied a voice behind them. "I like it. Shows a bit of initiative." Mr Byron had his arms crossed. "The only thing I'm intrigued to know is how both of you expect to execute such a project. You, Vonnegut: your plan seems very ambitious, if you don't mind me saying."

"Not really, sir. I've made feelies before, sir. On the ships orbiting the Fourth. It was one of the things they taught us, sir, because they wanted us to make our own entertainment. It was too expensive to bring all the equipment from Earth, see, so we just, you know, had to do it. I don't even need the latest programs. I'll improvise."

"I see." Mr Byron, who had a hologram of a bear cub on the lapel of his jacket, wafted back a wave of dangling hair and turned to Aurora. "And you, my sweet princess, goddess of the sunrise, how were you hoping to find authentic information on the school in the past now that our library has been deemed out of bounds to all but the Magistrate?"

"Ah." Aurora's face dropped. "You're right. I don't know, sir."

Mr Byron stroked his narrow chin. "You could always seek out ex-students of the school? Staff? Alumni, perhaps? People who might be able to tell you their stories? Of how the school was then? In the past?"

"Yes, sir," Aurora replied. "But I don't really know anyone."

"Oh, well there's old Mr Cauldhame, for example. He still lives in the village."

"Who's Mr Cauldhame?" Charlie and Aurora asked at the same time.

"He was once Head Boy here and later a Master. An interesting chap. Lives in a small cottage near the *Admiral Benbow* which he calls The Wasp Factory. Very close to the south exit."

"The Wasp Factory?" Aurora wrinkled her nose.

"What's a wasp?" asked Charlie.

"Extinct animal," Aurora said.

"Actually, they were insects," corrected Byron. "Technically speaking."

"What's an insect?" Charlie asked.

Aurora narrowed her eyes. "An extinct organism." She was conscious Mr Byron and Charlie were staring at her. "Cold-blooded. No legs. They moved by slithering."

"That would be a snake," Mr Byron said, stroking his chin. "Close but no cigar."

"What's a snake?" asked Charlie.

"Going back to the matter in hand," Mr Byron said, holding his arms wide open. "Sam – Mr Cauldhame – has an odd sense of humour, as you'll no doubt find out for yourselves – but I'm sure he would be happy to help you with your project. Do you want me to sign a release paper so you can go out of bounds and see him?"

Charlie looked at Aurora, and they both turned to Mr Byron and nodded like eager puppies.

XII

Athy saw Mrs Mallowan coming downstairs as she walked down to the first landing. The Headmistress winked at her as they came face to face. "The Ides of March have come, Athy."

"But not gone," Athy replied sadly.

"Ah, you're impossible." Mrs Mallowan cocked her head to one side. "Are you coming to the meeting?"

"Yes, I suppose I am."

"Come along then."

As they came downstairs to the main hall, they saw a roaring fire ablaze in the great chimney. The crackling of the flames almost drowned out the noise of the rain pelting the windows.

"Oh, it's too warm," Mrs Mallowan declared, walking on down the corridor.

Athy let her pass, pausing a moment to look at the fire. She remembered being in this very hall with her own parents, and Kizzie, many, many years before, when they'd first come to the school. She would never have imagined that day that she would stay here all these years, become part of the furniture, part of the architecture. Back then the school had seemed something terrifying, some kind of castle, full of gothic terrors.

"We're ready, Ma'am Jull-Costa," a prefect called out, and Athy shuffled down the hall to the Eleusinian Room, finding it full: packed to the gills with every type of human life-form the school had to offer. Mrs Mallowan was alone on the raised stage, standing in front of her golden throne, calling for calm. The doors were closed and the Headmistress bent down to talk to a cyborg who'd approached the stage.

"What's that idiot doing?" Chor-Zor, standing to the side of the stage, whispered to Row-Lin and Pull-Mun who were by his side.

Pull-Mun was nervous. "Is he telling Mallowan about what

we're going to do?"

"Relax, relax, both of you," Row-Lin responded, whispering so only they could hear. "Look at Ma'am Mallowan, she's nodding and smiling. It's nothing to do with us."

"When the study droid approaches her, that's the sign," Chor-Zor stated.

Row-Lin nodded. After she'd read the messages Pull-Mun had showed her, she'd finally made up her mind to do what Chor-Zor had been planning. They needed to remove Mrs Mallowan now, before all this silliness – this playing at being a Queen – got even more out of hand. In the end the decision had been a simple one for Row-Lin: what was more important: the school or friendship? Obviously the school. The school had been here when none of them had been here, and the school would go on after they'd gone. It was a painful but simple decision in the end.

"Look at her, how she acts," Chor-Zor hissed.

"Oh, wonderful Headmistress," the cyborg was saying, bending down on one knee before Mrs Mallowan. "Please tell us the curfew will be lifted tonight."

"Of course it won't!" Mrs Mallowan replied. "There are rules for a reason." She looked up at the school. "What would it be like if the stars chose a different path every night? Or the Moon? Or the sun? Why there would be chaos in the heavens! And the same goes for the Earth; for the school. I make rules for us to follow because they are for the good of the school. These rules are absolute. They are to guide you. I am here to guide you!"

The cyborg grovelled away backwards.

"Here comes the droid," whispered Chor-Zor. "Are you ready?"

"Ready," said Pull-Mun.

"It must be done," Row-Lin added, not without sadness.

All three took a step forwards.

Mrs Mallowan, on stage, noticed a dark movement behind the shining lid of the study droid and when she saw the three mods approaching, flattening out into a line, she knew exactly what they were going to do.

Chor-Zor lifted his scarlet, fizzing knife first, holding it under his cloak so nobody but Mrs Mallowan could see it. "This knife speaks for me," he hissed, stepping forwards and plunging.

As the blade burned into her, Mrs Mallowan hardly moved. At the back of the room Athy slipped out. Some students stood up to see what was going on but there was a strange, eerie silence in the room. Row-Lin took a step forward now, her blade fizzing grey, also hidden, and as she drew back her elbow, preparing to strike, Mrs Mallowan shook her head.

"Oh, not you, too, my darling friend?"

Row-Lin closed her eyes as she struck.

Mrs Mallowan looked down to watch the blade enter her chest. "So this is how it ends."

Pull-Mun, who was trembling, stepped over the falling body of Mrs Mallowan and used his own blade, thinner and sharper and bluer than the others, and stabbed down into her back three times. He dropped his cloak on top of the body and turned to the room. "She has collapsed!"

"Liberty! Freedom! Tyranny is dead!" Chor-Zor announced from the stage.

The Magistrate reacted with confusion and shock, coming to life as they realised that what they were watching was not some kind of prank or act: their Headmistress was dead. Some ran for the doors.

"Tell everyone in the school!" Chor-Zor shouted. "Spread the word!"

Row-Lin came to join him at the front of the stage. She raised her arms and voice. "Do not be afraid, everyone," she began, and they listened. "Please! Do not run away." As the students and teachers turned to look at her, she went on: "This was a debt that Mrs Mallowan had to pay for being so ambitious. Her fear and guilt killed her. This has nothing to do with any of you. It was for the good of the school, nothing more. It is done, now. The debt is paid and the wrong has been righted. It is good she died today, here, with us, like this."

The speech seemed to work and there was, immediately, some calm and order. The mods around the hall and the chief human prefects now stood up at the end of the lines of chairs and began to help the others file out in an orderly fashion. It was almost as if everyone knew what had happened must happen but no one quite believed it. They had entered the room in one mood, in one school, and now everything had changed. They were in a different mood, in a different school: they were all different people. Some of those who looked back at Mrs Mallowan, where she lay, broke into tears.

"Where is Ma'am Athy?" Chor-Zor asked, looking through the departing bodies.

"She left," a cyborg student with a vicious electronic lisp told him.

"There are people going mad out there," reported a human student, a Consul, whose face was pale and sickly. He had come running in from the dome. "There's chaos!"

"As, of course, there must be," Row-Lin replied. She was perfectly calm and composed, and radiated righteousness. "Who knows what fate has in store for us all. The only thing that we know is that all of us must die one day."

"If you die early," Chor-Zor said, grinning, "you save yourself a lot of worry."

"In that case we did Mrs Mallowan a favour," Row-Lin replied. She turned to Chor-Zor and Pull-Mun and told them: "This act of ours will become famous, you know. It is part of history now. People in other schools and other countries will talk of it in other languages. We have made history here today and we must go out there now and proclaim this to the people."

"We must be strong," Pull-Mun agreed. "We have done right. She deserved to die."

"We have done a great deed," Chor-Zor said.

"I agree," Row-Lin concluded. "But let's not waste any more time in here. Let's go out there and convince the school."

Behind them, on the stage, lay Mrs Mallowan, covered with a black cape.

XIII

"Have you ever used one of these before?" Mr Banks asked Alice.

"Not this model but similar."

"You've flown a Nano then?"

"Yes."

Mr Banks clapped his hands and his eyes fired in and out happily. "Obviously we're all up to date with the security and our failsafe systems have been protocol-verified but, even so, I do have to remind you of the dangers you face in taking part in an experiment like this."

"Yes, Mr Banks. Don't worry, I understand. Thanks for the warning." Alice smiled. "Lucky you don't have to get my parents' permission, really."

"Yes." The teacher wasn't sure whether to laugh. "Right, well, do not disengage from the machine at any time, please. Always remain in the system as long as it's connected. You know the basics: stick to them. We don't want any surprises."

"Yes, sir."

"If you disengage before we're switched off you know you run the risk of staying in there. Of never coming back." Mr Banks held out his arms. "Whichever way you look at it, that would not be a laughing matter."

"Yes, sir, I know."

"Good. Well, then. Let's get started."

Alice pulled a face as she squashed the headpiece, which looked like a black astronaut's helmet, down over her hair. Roald, sitting next to her, was already lit up, the dark screen on his visor flashing with bright pink sparks and fizzing shapes. His job was more difficult than hers but far less physically risky: he would not be connected to the system, only to Alice and the screens. Whatever happened, he could always come back to the dome at any moment.

"You can use your hands, of course," Mr Banks said, slipping the gloves over Alice's fingers, "but as I'm sure you know, you'll move the Nani much faster and more accurately if you only use your mind. Thought is much quicker than action after all."

"Can someone light me up?" Alice's voice was transmitted to the classroom through wall-speakers. "I'm blind in here."

"Illumination in three, two, one," Roald told her, his voice close and ticklish in her ear.

The Nani's dashboard came up in front of Alice's eyes. She heard her own heartbeat and the weird crackle of her nervous system. *Tune it out*, she told herself. *Do what you were taught to do. Concentrate on the Nani.*

The Nani was a tiny robot spaceship, so small you could land over a thousand on the full stop on the end of this sentence. In day-to-day life, in most human colonies in the solar system, Nanis were used for medical procedures: medics could locate problems by thought-flying Nanis through patients' bodies. The Nanis at St Francis were larger and bulkier than medical or military ones, but still state-of-the-art.

Nani Technology (or 'Tanc', as the children called it) was a standard subject in schools and Alice had been flying them for as long as she could remember. In the old days they'd taken trips as classes, on cigar-shaped vessels which sailed down veins and through organs. These days children flew themselves, although most flights were strictly controlled; the routes and machinery measured and bound by laws and norms.

Security was the biggest problem: there was always the risk that a Nani could take the personality – the brain – of the person using it with it if it became disconnected from the control systems. But as long as the user – or flyer, as they were called – remained in contact with the central controls via the gloves and helmet, there was little danger. The only real accidents of note had occurred when nature had intervened: earthquakes on Mars shaking fliers loose, or meteors suddenly striking classrooms during experiments on the Moon.

Most schools and parents thought the advantages of using Nani technology outweighed the dangers. Students with Nani experience found better jobs. Campaigners also pointed out that in the far past, students had worked with fire or chemicals, gas and electricity, and although there had been accidents, it had been thought advantageous and educational. One could die at any moment of any day, was the argument.

Alice lifted her head so she could see under her helmet and gave a thumbs up to Mr Banks who was standing by to launch. The Nani carried a camera – now showing the enormous, thick forest of hairs on Alice's pink earlobes – and was also connected to Roald's screens and the main viewing portals in the classroom.

"All clear for launch," Roald announced.

"Give me a few minutes to make the flight up into the brain," Alice told him. "Before switching everything on. Save some energy for the party."

"Keep concentrating on the basics, Alice," Mr Banks reminded her. "We don't want to fire too much memory activity just yet."

"Roger that, sir," Alice replied. She blinked twice with her right eye and – as was standard – flight data began scrolling along the top of the screen inside her helmet. It gave velocity, height, temperature, coverage, route information and system warnings.

The Nani carried several tools and odd technological items but the children and Mr Banks had removed all but the core features for the flight that morning. They wanted the Nani to be able to hit maximum speed as their plan was to attempt to follow the birth of an idea on the brain's surface and no one knew how fast a new idea could travel. ("Nobody's ever been stupid enough to try to hitch a ride on an idea before," Roald had said.)

"Launch," said Alice.

"Launch," nodded Mr Banks, hand over the override.

"Launch," said Roald, and released the Nani.

Alice felt, as usual, a weird pain and heard a strange noise. It was like the sudden high-pitched ringing in the ears which happened from time to time with no warning. The pain was a headache: a flash of lightning. As usual a strange thought came with it: *when lightning flashes it is like a rip in the sky.* Alice saw herself very young, as a baby. She saw her mother's face leaning in to kiss her, a chain on her neck dangling. A horrible vision of monsters as trees, walking towards her, materialised.

"Alice!" shouted Roald.

Alice fought her way back to reality. "Here! Here!"

"Come back, get control," said Mr Banks in her ear, calmly. "You're flying. You're in. Concentrate only on what you can see. You're flying."

"I'm flying," said Alice. And there it was. The lovely view. *Keep your mind on one thing. The thing that you are doing right now. It's the hardest thing in the world to do but you must do it. Only think about what you are doing right now.*

"Coming out of the ear," Roald said. "In five, four, three..."

"There it is," Alice announced, as the screen showed a thick, gloopy smudge of material, like pea soup. Emerging from the gloom was a large mushroom head of coral: Alice's own brain. The closer she flew, banking to the right, gliding above the surface, the clearer the fissures and rift valleys became. When she looked down the deep, dark crevasses they seemed bottomless and made her shiver. "I'm going to head down to Section A."

"Roger that." Roald made a quick check of his own controls, revving and blink-starting the booster engines and rockets, as he would soon be taking over. Mr Banks had told them that as long as Alice was thinking about flying, they should be able to keep the main connections clear, but as soon as she started to think of anything abstract like memories or sudden ideas, Roald would have to take over.

The handover would be critical. Alice's mind would remain

connected but she would be in Roald's hands.

"Coming in low now," Alice said, her voice nervous. The screens buzzed to tell her they were over Section A of the cerebral cortex. Their target destination. "Approaching ACC now. All systems clear."

The Nani was low, just above the spongey planet of brain, sleeking over the vast, ridged surface. The brain itself looked dead, like a vegetable soaked too long in water, dribbling bubbles and dirt, but they all knew appearances could be deceiving.

"Switch to electro, please," Alice said.

"Switching to electro," echoed Roald.

Mr Banks, standing nearby, nervously chewed the skin by a nail. He'd lost Nanis in those ravines before and a crash could mean a lot of trouble from the higher-ups. These days they were looking for any excuse to replace human teachers with mods.

The switch from normal vision to electro, which meant all the electrical and neuron-based activity taking place in the vicinity of the Nani came up on screen, was like switching from black and white to colour. A dynamic, vivid, electric-hued firework display lit up Alice and Roald's eyeballs.

"The brightest, freshest yellow sparks are what we are looking for," Mr Banks reminded them, realising they needed help. "Check for the telltale fizz. A whirl in the middle of your visor indicates a memory; the speed of the whirl indicates how true and vivid the memories are. Arrowing sparks, the shooting stars, are inspiration – they're coming from external sources, what Alice is seeing and hearing and smelling. If one of them turns purple or blue and crosses a whirl, you get in there."

"Roald, you'd better take over," Alice said. She could feel herself starting to think about Mars already. Sometimes she thought her own brain raced ahead of her: it knew about things before she did. Mr Banks said this was normal, that there was a part of the brain which was thinking about, anticipating and planning for the future, and sometimes this part of the brain was dominant.

"Roger that," came Roald's voice.

"Here we go then."

Alice closed her eyelids and a thousand memories assaulted her.

She thought of her mother and wanted to cry but she didn't want to share her mother and her sadness with the class, not even with Roald. Her sadness was for her alone and so she fought the memory and suppressed it, even though she could hear Roald saying he had something. Instead she quickly fixated on a school trip they'd once taken to Olympus Mons, the highest volcano in the solar system, on Mars.

Alice remembered the school ship – they'd flown from the space station – and how the walls of the ship had turned transparent as they'd approached the huge, kilometres-high cliffs which ringed the volcano. Such steep cliffs; escarpments, rusty red against the grey sky. And that long, long, long slope of the volcano: an enormous, rising, massive slope going up, up, up to the caldera. You didn't notice the height you were going when the slopes were so shallow, the black sky so alive with stars above.

"Got it!" shouted Roald and fired his javelins into the fiery, spinning circle of lurid colours. "Hit! I have it. Tagged it! We're on an idea!"

The Nani jerked forwards – both Roald and Alice screamed – and Mr Banks, outside, placed his palm over the emergency stop control. "Are you two all right?"

"Woooah!" screamed Roald as the Nani zipped forwards behind Alice's idea, their visors shaking with the strain of keeping up at the same speed.

"We're riding it!" Alice whispered, exhilarated. In her mind she concentrated hard on the memory. That day they had flown right over the top of the mountain: the highest mountain humans had ever seen. The enormous, gaping lava holes had stared up at them from under their feet while the Martian plains had spread out to every horizon like a vast copper carpet.

"Hang on, both of you!" Mr Banks called out. "Keep calm! Keep it under control!"

"We're going down!" Roald shouted as the Nani dived deep into a brain crevasse. Only the fizzing light on their visors told them they were moving at all: it was like a star in the middle of the screen, moving ever so slightly, jagging from left to right. Even the juddering had lessened. They might have stopped.

"What's happened?" Alice began.

"We've caved," Roald said quietly. "We're in a deep cave. Stay calm."

Mr Banks turned as a pupil drew his attention to a group of senior students from the Magistrate whom he'd just noticed standing at the classroom door. "Yes? What is it?" he asked. "Can't you see we're busy?"

"Bad news, sir," one of them said.

"Just a moment." Mr Banks turned to the controls and told Alice and Roald: "We're going to have to abort the mission, I'm afraid. You both did spectacularly well, but I'm afraid we must stop."

"But, sir!" Alice cried. "Not now! Let's see where the idea goes!"

"But nothing." Mr Banks hit the override, the idea was released, and the Nani immediately rose back up the dark hole to pop out into the green bubbling soup where the brain lay.

Alice's skin was sizzling. She was wet with sweat. "Oh, no."

"You both did very well," Mr Banks told them. "Look up the data on the brain crevasses. Ask yourself why the idea seemed to want to dive back into the brain. It's there in the guides. I want your Mission Report by tomorrow."

"What happened, sir?" asked Roald, reeling in the javelins and switching back to normal vision. "Change screens," he told Alice, who was looking out at the gloomy, spongey brain disappearing into the jade gloom.

"Screens changed," Alice replied. "You fly us back, Roald. I'm exhausted."

"I have to go," Mr Banks told them. He'd spotted, looking down through the dome walls, through the gloomy yellow sky, Chor-Zor, Pull-Mun and Row-Lin marching down the tunnel from the Main Building. "Something's happened."

"What is it, sir?" asked Roald, coming across to look down too.

Mr Banks shook his head. "Trouble."

XIV

Athy creaked more than the stairs as she came down to join the nervous but strangely quiet crowds gathering in the entrance hall. The tunnel entrance to the dome and the corridor to the Eleusinian Room were both blocked by modified teachers.

As the news passed between them, the students looked confused more than sad. Poor Ma'am Mallowan had suffered a fatal heart attack, Athy heard someone say. She had collapsed during the Magistrate's meeting. The mods had done all they could to save her but nothing had worked. Mr Chor-Zor had taken over as Headmaster and was directing matters, making sure calm was restored. Ma'am Mallowan was very old. It was natural. The medics were here. Everything must be controlled to restore order.

How scared we all are of death and dying, Athy thought, walking into the crowd. *What a fascinating hold it has over us. People treat death as something supernatural though it's the most natural thing in the world. Birth and life are far less predictable and possible than death ever could be but death has a kind of magic. It awes us.*

Athy moved through the crowd like a ghost. Without noticing her, the green-uniformed students parted as she passed by. Those that did see her bowed their heads. They knew Ma'am Athy must be feeling what had happened to Ma'am Mallowan on a deeper level than they all were. The old lady had known Ma'am Mallowan for years, after all.

"Sorry, miss," someone said.

Instead of thanking them, as she knew she should, Athy replied: "Yes. So am I."

Passing down the corridor, ignoring the mod who tried weakly to stop her, Athy saw the door of the Eleusinian Room was open and stepped inside.

There was Mrs Mallowan, lying on the low, raised stage at

the far end of the room, covered with a purple sheet, her arms and legs folded strangely under her. Around her were mods and some St Francis' students, kneeling. There were no tears. People were sad but nobody, it was obvious now, had ever really loved the woman. Mrs Mallowan had been a leader who had commanded respect. But now she had gone people were thinking of themselves. Thinking of the school, perhaps, too, but most of all thinking of their own security, their own futures. The atmosphere in the room, Athy sensed, was of nobody wanting to rock the boat. Of them all wanting to get this woman buried and to get on with things and get everything back to normal.

Mr Chor-Zor, whose features seemed older somehow, his eyebrows flecked with grey, his fingers interlocked like a wizard's within his black gown sleeves, his voice low and serious, came over to greet her.

"Athena, Athena, Athena. What can I say? What can we say? Such a sad day for the school. But she didn't suffer, you saw that. It all happened so very quickly, just as the meeting started. We hardly had a chance to say a word. But, you know, I think if she could have chosen anywhere for this to happen, she would have chosen for it to happen here." He wafted his sleeve about the room – the library, the school flags, the panelled walls and high ceiling.

"My congratulations on your promotion to Headmaster."

"Oh, that's temporary," Chor-Zor replied after a beat. "Protocol. Until we can have a proper meeting to make a further decision."

I was joking, Athy wanted to say, shocked that Chor-Zor had taken her so seriously. So this was how it was going to be. She couldn't help noticing that he had made his face paler: the mods probably had a setting called *Grieve*.

Medics were working on the body in outdoor breathing apparatus and looking up they began to call for the room to be cleared. Chor-Zor gave an order and the other mods snapped to attention. Soon only Athy, Chor-Zor, the medics and Mrs Mallowan's body were left in the room.

Athy walked across to look down at the body and, as the medics worked, she caught sight of what had really happened to Mrs Mallowan. Just as she suspected, this had been no heart attack. Somehow the mods had cleaned the blood from the floor and managed to cover the worst of the scars before the students had been let in but Athy could see what they'd done to Mrs Mallowan as clearly as if her old friend was lying there telling her.

Don't worry, Athy thought, looking down at Mrs Mallowan's closed eyes. *I'll make sure everyone finds out what really happened.*

"Do you have any plans for the funeral?" she asked Chor-Zor, turning away from the medics who wanted to shift Mrs Mallowan on to the stretcher hovering unsupported in the air nearby.

"I thought we might make some speeches in Assembly tomorrow morning." Chor-Zor scanned Athy's face for a sign, any sign, that she had seen the wounds. The truth.

"Surely St Catherine's would be more appropriate?" asked Athena. St Catherine's was the local place of worship, connected by tunnel to the school. Religion these days – any religion – was a controversial subject. Modifieds considered all religions and spirituality akin to superstition and for the last few years the old church had fallen into ruins. But it seemed the appropriate place, still, for a human funeral.

"No. Too dangerous. Structurally." Chor-Zor held up a hand to indicate to Athy that she should leave. "The speeches will be made at the end of Assembly tomorrow."

"May I talk during the Assembly?"

For the first time Chor-Zor's face changed. He dropped the act. "Yes, of course. As long as, like everyone else, you follow protocol. No more than two minutes. Keep it respectful. Nothing to incite problems. We want the changeover to be as smooth as possible for all concerned, for the good of the school."

"Yes, of course you do."

"Sir," purred Chor-Zor.

Athy raised an eyebrow. "I beg your pardon?"

"I am the Headmaster now, Ma'am Athy. You will address me with the correct title. Sir or Headmaster."

"I see." Athy bowed her head. "Sir."

"You have my permission to join us on the stage for Assembly."

"Thank you so much, Headmaster. Very kind."

"See you tomorrow, then."

After Athy had shuffled out, with one last glance at Mrs Mallowan, Mr Pull-Mun, who had stayed back to assist the medics, came over to Chor-Zor. "Do you think that's wise, sir?"

"What?" asked Chor-Zor, distracted.

"Letting her speak at the Assembly tomorrow?"

Chor-Zor shrugged. "She's a survivor. And a friend. She'll not say anything to harm us or herself. She's too old in the tooth for that. She knows not to say anything controversial or anything that'll cause trouble."

"How can you be so sure?"

Chor-Zor nodded at the stretcher passing by. "Because now she knows what will happen if she does."

XV

"Is that old lady up there really your aunty?" asked Aurora.

She and Charlie were sitting in the middle of the crowd of mumbling, muttering children waiting for Assembly to start. The entire school were packed into the dome that morning, all in uniform, all aware that something had happened to Mrs Mallowan.

"My great-aunt, actually," corrected Charlie. As he smoothed down his hair a droplet of water trickled off the end of his nose and he licked it off.

"Urr!" Aurora replied, shocked. "I can't believe you just did that!"

"I can touch my nose with my tongue. Lick bogeys out. Can you?"

"You're a disgusting pig! Really!"

Charlie laughed hard.

It was bright inside the dome. The central waterfalls were tinkling and fake birdsong twittered from above the massed heads. The highest, curved roof panels somehow converted the foul, yellow air from outside into bright, old-fashioned sunshine and accompanying this came wafts of greenness, wet earth and cut grass. Despite the solemn circumstances, the students were in good spirits.

"I told you naturalisation would work," Row-Lin whispered to Pull-Mun, who was sitting beside her on the raised stage. She was talking about the artificial smells they were pumping into the domes. The teachers were all in formal dress: black flowing capes and silver mortar-board hats. Row-Lin looked stunningly fierce. Her long ponytail had been knotted into a tight bun and her lips were scarlet and pursed.

"Amazing how sensitive humans are to even the tiniest atmospheric changes," replied Pull-Mun in a low, quiet voice.

He was displaying a new clean-shaven, solemn look. He had selected a particularly deep, respectful shade of brown for his eyeballs but still looked weak. In the end it was difficult, even for mods, to change or escape their default personality settings.

Alice was slumped in a seat five rows from the stage, snivelling. She hadn't slept well – she'd had vivid, bad dreams and her bones ached from the inside out. After Assembly she would go to see a matron-medic. The last thing she felt like doing was being here or going to classes.

"You not up for having another go with the Nani today?" Roald asked her. He was pale with grief but strangely calm. The worst thing that could possibly have happened had happened and now he felt numb. He didn't want to be alone.

"I peel so bad," Alice sniffled. "I'm sorry, Roald, but I cah't." Her nose glowed comically red. She had her arm interlocked with Roald's: she felt so sorry for the boy.

"You actually do look terrible."

"Fank you." Alice blew her nose. "I fink."

Roald looked back up to the stage and began counting the panels on the dome ceiling. He counted anything – counting was the only thing that stopped him crying. Counting was the only thing that stopped him getting angry or screaming. How strange that everything, in some way, seemed like a joke. At any moment his grandmother was going to jump up from behind the stage and yell, "Surprise!" Yes, it all seemed like one great, practical joke.

Mrs Mallowan's body was covered by a purple sheet, balanced on a small scaffold to one side of the stage where the teachers were sitting. Holograms of flowers fluttered across the coffin's scrolling screens. The dead Headmistress' grey hair had been neatly combed but it was all in the wrong place, the wrong way around somehow.

She looks nothing like herself, Athy thought, looking sideways from her seat. *She'd be so embarrassed*. Mrs Mallowan had always been so contentious about how she looked. *Oh, I know what they've done – they've put a wig on her!*

Athy couldn't help smiling at the irony of it: the woman who'd always been so meticulous about how she looked in public now looked ridiculous with all the school there, watching her. But this feeling soon transmuted into anger. *They murdered her and they couldn't even put her wig on properly. They murdered her and now they're making her look ridiculous in front of the very people she worked so hard to impress and lead.*

To a general hush and with all eyes focussing upon him, Mr Chor-Zor walked up to the lectern and looked out over the rows of faces. "Students, teachers and fellow followers of the truth," he began, his voice amplified and echoey, cape settling.

The modified master waited for the shuffling and muttering to stop. Birdsong and tinkling water sounds filled the quiet.

Chor-Zor silently crossed to where Mrs Mallowan's coffin was floating above its scaffold. "Children, fellow members of staff: if anyone here thinks they loved Ma'am Mallowan more than me, I would ask them to raise their hands now."

Nobody moved. The birdsong was silenced, mid-tweet. Only the fans whirring behind the ventilator shafts could be heard, a sound so usual to those gathered there that morning that only Charlie, Alice and a few other new arrivals noticed it. It was a deep, rumbling hum.

"What happened to Ma'am Mallowan yesterday was a terrible accident, my friends. An awful, though natural, occurrence. Today we grieve. When things like this happen in this life – in this short, precious life that we are given – there are always two ways of responding: with positivity or negativity. And I say that today we grieve and we pay our respects knowing that tomorrow we rise. It is what Ma'am Mallowan would have wanted. It is what she would have expected. And it is what we will do."

Some heads were nodding, some sleeves fluttering. From

mid-crowd, a cough. Those on the stage were aware of blurs in the lights at the back of the dome: more latecomers pushing through from the tunnel.

"You see, my friends, we can view what happened to Ma'am Mallowan yesterday as an end or a new beginning. I see it as the beginning of a bright future. What happened yesterday will allow our school to live the future which all of you deserve, and must live.

"Would you rather we had continued as we were, slaves to an outdated system which needed changing, which was holding us back? Or would you rather our beloved Ma'am Mallowan passed on naturally, like her system, to leave us, as we are now, free to face the future we deserve?"

The students looked blankly back at Chor-Zor but many of the teachers were nodding – and not just the modifieds.

"As I loved Ma'am Mallowan, so I weep for her today.

"She was brave and she was our leader and I rejoice in her inspiration; in her leadership of the school. But it's also true – and in times like this we must be honest! – that she was stubborn, blocking and darkening what we see as our perfect future."

"Perfection," Pull-Mun said, in a voice which carried. He had his chin down, black arms folded on his chest, booted feet stretched out and was nodding as if a grave universal truth had been spoken.

"All together we are the spirit of the school," Chor-Zor went on, voice rising. "All together! Not one! Not alone!"

"Together to perfection," chimed Row-Lin, hands clasped, also seemingly convinced about the truth of all this. She nodded fiercely, looking around, blinking furiously. *This was sad*, she was saying with her body, *but necessary*.

Chor-Zor balled a fist. "Yes, there are tears and sadness – there must be! But now, when we look ahead, we must see light, not darkness. We must see perfection!"

"Progress," came a human voice. Humans preferred the

word 'progress' to 'perfection'. The human teachers thought perfection was an idea that you strived towards while the modifieds believed perfection was an achievable state.

"Is there really anyone here who doesn't want the best for our school?" Chor-Zor asked. "Is there really anyone here who wants to stay in the darkness? To not be in the light?"

"Nobody," someone agreed – a pupil's voice – and there came more voices, old and young.

Chor-Zor pointed in the direction of these voices and nodded, waving his gloves. "Yes, yes! Don't be afraid to speak up! Of course you don't! No! You ask why the events of yesterday happened and I tell you they *had to* happen. The future of this school cannot and will not be stopped!"

A burst of scattered applause.

"I shall step down now," Chor-Zor said, turning to point to Athena, "And let Ma'am Athy speak." He waited for a reaction to this news, which never really came, but said, anyway: "Yes, yes. It is only fair that we hear from those with differing views from our own. The old ways can sometimes be useful to us."

Mrs Jull-Costa stood up but Chor-Zor immediately turned back to the school and continued, leaving Athy standing, stranded: "I will finish by telling you all solemnly, then, that if I ever stand in the way of the future of this wonderful institution, I would expect you all to do exactly the same thing to me as we must do to Ma'am Mallowan.

"We give thanks, we pay our respects but onwards we move – towards the light. Always towards the light of perfection!"

"To the light!" came back the voices.

"To perfection!" Chor-Zor finished, and shook both hands in the air as the students and teachers warmly applauded him.

"Live, sir! Lead us to that bright future!"

"Follow the new Headmaster to perfection!"

"Who can't want perfection?"

"Master Chor-Zor is the future! He sees it clearly! He can

take us there!"

"To the light!"

"Perfection!"

Athy, who had remained standing, smiling sadly, now walked up to the edge of the stage and looked out at the faces. Once upon a time of course, she had sat among them, a young girl in a green uniform, later as a young teacher with darker hair and a sharper mind. Yes, she had been here before but she had never felt quite like she did now. Her whole body was buzzing with a queer force of energy: there was a spirit inside her which she knew must be heard. She had made a promise to Mrs Mallowan in the Eleusinian Room which she intended to keep.

"Friends, lovers of the truth, schoolmates, colleagues and all good, honest beings," she began. Her voice was surprisingly strong despite the amplification system having been switched off after Chor-Zor's speech. "I ask you to please listen to me for a moment."

She waited patiently for silence.

"I have come here today to bury Ma'am Mallowan, not to praise her."

Athy looked across at the body of her old friend and foe, and for a moment she was genuinely moved. She accepted, suddenly, that Mrs Mallowan was gone and saw her as a child again, a young woman, a fierce fighter, a friend who'd gone for long walks with her when long walks were still possible. Athy saw the life entire of the other woman flash before her eyes. *We only really become who we are when we are gone because it's only then that it's all finished, that it's all over*, she thought.

"Come on, Aunty," Charlie whispered, watching. He was nervously biting his fingernails.

"I want to say something else," Athy began again, turning back to face them, and there was a release of tension in the dome. She raised a finger. "The evil that people do lives on after they die. The good is buried with them."

"Here she goes," whispered Pull-Mun, shaking his head.

"Leave her," hissed Row-Lin. "She can't do any harm. Just let her have her say."

Athy looked out at the school. "Master Chor-Zor has just told you that Ma'am Mallowan was blocking the future of the school, darkening its way. If that's true, it was a terrible thing to do and my, oh, my how she has paid for it. Thanks to Master Chor-Zor and the other modified teachers you see here behind me bowing their heads, Ma'am Mallowan has certainly paid for darkening the future! Yes, she has. She has paid with her life!"

The atmosphere changed and there was some nervous shuffling from among the watching bodies. A cough. A change in the temperature though the vents still hummed.

"Ma'am Mallowan brought new technology into St Francis. It was *she* who introduced modified teachers like Ms Row-Lin, her great friend." Athy looked back at Row-Lin and smiled in a horrible way: *Are you proud of what you've done?* she seemed to ask. "It was Ma'am Mallowan," she went on, turning back to the school, "who brought Master Chor-Zor and his friends here and it was *she* who oversaw the building of this dome. Was she blocking our way then? Was she blocking the future?

"Although Ma'am Mallowan had known for some time that many of the modified teachers were not happy with their status, that they believed they are somehow better than human beings, did she expel them from the school or remove them from their posts? Did she block their futures? No, she didn't. Because she knew that they were important to the school's future, to all of your futures. She wanted this to be a school for everyone! For everyone – all people, all beings!"

But suddenly, after a minute or two of appearing so determined and focussed, Athy seemed to become aware of being overwhelmed by where she was and what she was doing. As a mixture of strong feelings flowed through her, her face crumpled up and she broke down. How terrible was it when you lost someone? Where did they go? And that they would never come back! Oh, that awful feeling – *nobody* is strong enough to resist tears in the face of it. "Oh, this is a such a terrible thing that has happened!"

"She's right!" someone called out from the pews.

"They must know the truth," Athy said to herself.

"Sit down, Aunt Athy," Charlie hissed, squirming in discomfort.

"Yesterday," Athy, just about in control of herself, said, determined to go on. "Yesterday, we might have been able to hear Ma'am Mallowan's wise words from her own mouth. She might have been able to defend herself, to explain her vision for the future – but not anymore." Athy pointed at the hovering corpse. "Look how she is now. Look how capable she is of speaking, of defending herself today."

"It was an accident," Chor-Zor sighed, fluttering his artificial eyebrows and shaking his shiny head. "A natural occurrence!"

"This was *not* natural," Athy snapped back, walking across Mrs Mallowan's coffin and placing a hand on her old friend's hair. Turning to the school, she continued:

"The first time I met this lady, she explained to me that we were at a crucial moment in human history and the history of the school. For the first time, human beings were capable of improving themselves with technology, of mixing technology and biology to create modified people – a great race of humans who would make humanity better than ever, who would create a brighter world."

Athy was shaking with emotion and this emotion silenced everyone.

"But we all know that wasn't quite how it worked out. As good as technology is, there is no way yet to reproduce our intricate brains. Technology hasn't yet caught up with nature and Ma'am Mallowan knew this. She knew that what was needed, to guarantee a safer future, was *balance*. She knew that to create a better world we need to work together in harmony, in balance – that people work best, and have always worked best when they work *together*. Isn't that what our history has shown us? What the best of humanity shows us? Our great buildings and art and cities and ideas?

"Yes, her dream was balance and harmony. *That* was her dream for the school. That we would all work together; that the future would be better for all of us, not just for some. *That* was her future – and it was a bright one."

Athy lifted Mrs Mallowan's grey hand from the coffin and kissed it. Hands shot to mouths and Pull-Mun seemed about to stand up until Chor-Zor lifted his arm and called for calm.

Athy went on, face rigid: "That idea was dealt a blow yesterday. And these people you see behind me here today have decided that they know better. They talk of Mrs Mallowan blocking the path to a brighter future but it is *they* who have dealt a blow to your future, for they have made *your* future *theirs*."

The modifieds, led by Chor-Zor, stood as one. "Enough!"

Under the dome, in various rows, arguing had broken out. Some students and teachers were standing, others shouting. Fists were being waved though it was not at all clear who was angry with whom and who was being threatened.

"Ma'am Mallowan and your future did not simply fall over and die of natural causes," Athy declared, pulling off the wig Mrs Mallowan was wearing, whipping away the purple sheet, to reveal the terrible injuries she had suffered at the hands of the mods. Her voice was loud, as clear as a war-siren. Nobody missed a word: "No! Here is the real blow to your future! Here are the real blows! Here is *your future – our future* – lying murdered!"

"Murder," someone shouted.

Athy draped the purple sheet around her neck and pointed at the dead body. "Let this be a sign of how these people work and what will happen to you if you, too, decide to stand in their way! These people represent disharmony! They are unbalanced! It is they who crave power and will do anything to achieve it!"

After a moment's pause, the dome descended into chaos.

XVI

Charlie stood on tiptoes, a lighthouse rising from the green sea of students breaking around him. The dome lights were flickering and, sometimes, the yellow sky was visible as it really was; the huge, low eye of the Moon too staring in. Over the students' excited babbling, the school speaker system was issuing instructions:

Return calmly to your homerooms!

Move immediately towards the Kwad!

Charlie thought he'd seen Aunty Athy tumbling off the stage at the very end of her speech but in the ensuing chaos he'd lost her. Before he'd been able to get to her, students had jumped up, chairs had gone over and there'd been a great rush for the exits at the back of the hall.

Charlie spotted Roald and swam against the tide towards him, shouting out, when he was close, for Alice. Roald gestured and pointed, telling Charlie she'd gone towards the Main Building and that he thought she'd had their aunt with her. Buoyed by this, Charlie pushed his way back into the centre of the crowd and went with the flow, eventually reaching the bottleneck at the back of the dome.

Move calmly to your homerooms!

Most students did as they were told and, as they came out of the dome, turned right and moved down into the long subterranean tunnel which led up to the Kwad. Garbled voices echoed off the walls as everyone tried to tell everyone else about what they thought had happened. Charlie spotted Alice standing against the far wall near the tunnel entrance – he recognised her pink headband – and pushed himself over to where she was.

"I think Aunt Athy tried to get back to her flat," Alice told him when he got there. She had stopped to get her breath back. "I'm pretty sure I saw her going down the tunnel there." She pointed at the clear-roofed passageway which led to the Main Building. Mouthfuls of dirt and loose topsoil were being spat against the scratched ceiling tiles by fresh, angry waves of wind rearing up outside.

"Did you actually *see* her?"

"No, the stage collapsed. Everyone around me went crazy. If it wasn't for Roald covering me I think I would have got crushed too."

"The same as me, then." Charlie shrugged. "I guess the only thing we can do is check if she did go back to her flat."

They waded through the crowd and walked together down the steps to the short, empty corridor, conspicuous suddenly. Strictly speaking there was no reason why they shouldn't go to the Main Building at that time – they might have needed to see a teacher or even their great-aunt – but since the messages were continuing, ordering them to go to the Kwad, they both knew they would most likely have problems if they encountered any teachers, especially mods.

Thankfully there was no one at the doorway to the Main Building and the entrance hall was also deserted. Alice whispered, because it seemed the right thing to do. "Let's go upstairs. Try not to make any noise."

Although they tried to step only on the outside of each stair, the old wood creaked and groaned – sometimes agonisingly loudly – and there was no way they could get up them all without making noise. They'd made it to the top landing, though, when Charlie stopped and put his fingers to his lips. There was someone in their great-aunt's rooms, he motioned. He could hear the floorboards. "Hear it?" he asked his sister in a low voice.

Alice smiled. "She's all right!"

"Come on!"

But as they started to run down the passageway Chor-Zor's angry figure strode out of their aunt's doorway. He was speaking to someone behind him, his features dark and fierce

– he no longer had to pretend to be anything else – and this gave Alice and Charlie just enough time to jam themselves into a space between the wall and the side of an old cupboard.

"Tear this place apart!" Chor-Zor cried angrily as he passed. His soft-soles had been switched off: now he was wearing war boots. A phalanx of mods ran ahead and crashed down the stairs.

"Perhaps it wasn't Jull-Costa they saw coming up here?" asked Pull-Mun, hurrying to keep up with Chor-Zor, his boots just as noisy. His metal shoulder clattered against the cabinet the children were hiding beside.

"Find her!" Row-Lin shouted over the banisters. "*Find her!*"

Chor-Zor stopped at the top of the staircase, his black cape sweeping around behind him a moment later like a shadow. He turned and stared back down the corridor.

"What is it?" asked Row-Lin.

Chor-Zor's eyes disappeared as he went to full systems. "Life-forms."

Row-Lin and Pull-Mun came to stand on either side of Chor-Zor. "Two," Pull-Mun said.

"I have two also," agreed Row-Lin.

Charlie and Alice lay squeezed together in the half-shadows, hardly breathing.

"The cats," Chor-Zor muttered, real anger in his voice. "It's her cats."

"I'll kill them now," Pull-Mun decided, stepping forwards. He walked like a gorilla, hunched over, slightly forwards-leaning, knuckles turned outwards at his side.

"No, no. First her. Then them."

"The dome is emptied," Row-Lin reported, receiving a message.

"The Eleusinian Room?" Chor-Zor said. "Has anyone checked there?"

Charlie and Alice listened to the three mods clump noisily down towards the Main Hall. Gradually their bootsteps faded away.

"They're *so* angry," Alice said, laughing nervously, stepping out into the corridor. The door of the cupboard they'd been hiding behind creaked open and Alice saw it was filled with protection suits: those suits had saved them. A mewling from further down the corridor drew her attention to Romulus and Remus as the cats came snaking out of their aunt's rooms.

"Good," replied Charlie. "Did you see what they did to Mallowan? They're nothing but common murderers!"

Alice went to the cats, kneeling and stroking them as they brushed up against her. "See if there's any food inside, Charlie. They're starving."

Charlie went into his aunt's flat and knew immediately she wasn't there. He could sense the room was empty. Nevertheless, he looked out of the window and under the sofa and finally took a small container of food from on top of the fridge and, cracking it open, passed it down to his sister. The cats, hungry, pawed Alice.

"This place stinks," Alice said, watching the cats eat. "It's not good. Not good at all."

"It's their bed, look." Charlie pointed at the sofa. It was the only place in the room which the mods hadn't turned upside down. "It's so disgusting."

"Well, I can't face cleaning it now. I'll come back if we have time. We should find Aunt Athy. That's the main thing, the only thing we have to do."

"We'd better go," Charlie agreed. "We have to find her before the mods do."

"Should we take the cats?"

"No!"

"Then we're coming back for them. We can't leave them here in this mess."

Charlie wasn't sure but he knew what Alice was like. She'd never leave if he didn't agree. "Fine. But, come on. Let's go. We'll come back for them later."

They retraced their steps, past the cupboard they'd hidden behind and down to the next landing. Creeping around the bannisters Charlie pointed down an old, shadowy corridor lined with a dusty, threadbare lime-green carpet. Something about it drew his attention. "Where does that one lead?"

Alice shrugged. "How should I know?"

"Look," said Charlie. He pointed to a series of dainty footprints on the dusty carpet.

Both children bent down to look. "Could be her," Alice said. "But it could be anyone." She looked into the darkness. The corridor was short and narrow, with three old-fashioned wooden doors at the bottom, all closed.

"These footprints are fresh," whispered Charlie. He stood up. "Come on, let's have a look at what's down there."

Charlie leading the way, the children walked along the carpet on either side of the footprints.

The first door, nailed closed, had a sign which said, *Secretary's Office*. "These must have been the old school offices, before they moved everything to the dome," Charlie guessed.

A second door, also nailed closed and sealed with red glue, said, *Head's Office*.

The third was unmarked, but closed and sealed.

"The footprints stop here." Alice had to crouch down to see them. The prints seemed to lead right up to the panelled wall she was standing in front of.

"They don't go to any of the doors. It's like she just disappeared into the wall." Charlie pressed his hands against the panels until he noticed something right in front of his nose. "Look. There's something here. A picture, I think."

"We need light," Alice said. She took out her dorm key and used its tiny, built-in torch to send a small beam to where Charlie was pointing. "You're right. It's a painting." It was a small, dark painting in a bronze frame. "What's it of? It looks so small and detailed!"

"Romans, I think," Charlie answered, peering into the scene. "Ancient Earth history. It's soldiers. Someone on a throne."

As Alice moved the beam of light over the dark painting, the children took in the scene. It seemed to show the aftermath of a military victory. There was a castle smoking in the background. The victors were proud to a man, none prouder than their leader, dressed in red and sitting on a throne, the main character in the painting. "Charlie, look here." Alice was pointing at one of the faces in the background, behind the throne, lit up in a circle of torchlight.

"Oh wow, it's Aunt Athy," Charlie whispered as though he couldn't believe it. He smiled. "How did she get in there?"

All went dark. Alice had dropped the torch. "Damn!"

"Who's there?" The deep, electrified voice of a mod teacher boomed from the stair-end of the corridor.

Charlie, kneeling to look for the torch, felt his hand close around something cold and metallic. He slipped whatever it was into his pocket before straightening up.

"Don't make me repeat myself." A light shone brightly in their faces. "Identify yourselves!"

"Charlie and Alice Vonnegut," Charlie said, turning into the light, hands above his head. "We're lost! Which way are the homerooms?"

"It's just children," they both heard the modified say. Then, in a sterner, louder voice, it went on: "Come out now! You can't be in here."

XVII

"And then what happened?" Aurora asked, bowing her head so that it was very close to Charlie's. She looked down at her screen, pretending to work.

Charlie clocked where Mr Byron was and pushed his bottom lip up. "Nothing, really. That was it. They took us to a holding dorm and we were stuck there til breakfast this morning. No one told us anything. It was quite comfortable actually. Did anyone tell you anything?"

"Only that Chor-Zor is the new Headmaster. Nothing else."

"I heard people saying we'll have to leave. Humans, normal people, I mean."

"Nah." Aurora wrinkled her nose. "They can't do that."

"That's what I thought, but this guy – you know Zweig? – he was saying the mods can more or less do what they want."

"Oh, don't listen to Zweig. He's the most pessimistic person I've ever met."

"I know, but he seemed to know what he was talking about."

"He knows the sum total of," but Aurora stopped as Mr Byron's shadow fell across them. The monkey on his lapel chattered, seeming to laugh. "How are we getting on here, then?"

"Good," Charlie nodded, sniffing.

"Great!" agreed Aurora.

"That's excellent." Mr Byron waved a shimmering rectangle between their bowed heads. "I have your permit to go out of bounds. I'm sure I don't have to tell you how difficult that was to get, especially right now, with the situation being what it is."

"Why do we need it, sir?" Charlie asked, before Aurora could kick him to shut him up.

"To see Mr Cauldhame, of course," Aurora scolded. She shook her head at Mr Byron. "Sorry, sir. We're really concentrating hard on what we're doing this morning. Charlie is a bit distracted."

"I remember now, sir. Mr Cauldhame. The first Head Boy of the school."

"Not the first," Mr Byron corrected, trans-passing the shining card to Aurora's keyset. "But one of the most important. He should certainly be able to help you with your project."

"Thank you, sir."

"Thanks, sir."

"Ah, by the way, chaps." Mr Byron had a habit of addressing the students, male or female, as chaps. "You might want to power up your screen before using it. Rather hard to work on it while you've got it switched off."

Charlie and Aurora were allowed to walk out of the school grounds as long as they wore protection suits and masks. The permission card was worn in the buckle on Aurora's chest and they had no problem surfacing from the tunnel under the Kwad or exiting through the shield doors.

"Wow, the air is actually quite thick," Charlie said, his voice cackling and breathy in the girl's ear as they took their first steps outside. All was yellow and dense.

"Is it? I don't notice anymore. Look! You can see the NLCs as clear as day."

Both stood in the swirling, dark-vermillion mist, staring up at the huge Moon. Charlie pointed. "That long, grey compound there, bottom of the L by the crater to the south of Llaws City. I'm quite sure that's where we were." He waited for Aurora to answer and was surprised, looking around, to find she was upset. He could see the red rings around her eyes. "What's wrong?"

"That's where Dad is," she said.

Charlie looked up. "Are you afraid you might not be able to go?"

Aurora shrugged. "How am I supposed to get there?"

Charlie almost said, *I'll take you!* For a moment he felt it. Like he could. Like a certainty. "I can't believe they won't let you go.

Why did they stop you?"

"Oh, come on, there's no point talking about it – it's too depressing."

The village roads spread out like spiders' legs from the remains of the old church. The main traffic route was a superhighway about a hundred metres deep which bypassed the village altogether so, above ground, all was silent.

A few people lived in hub-hovels with purple and scarlet dome-roofs. Like icebergs, three-quarters of these houses lay out of sight, underground. There were no sleek, speedy ships here, only sturdy, unspectacular high-altitude shuttles which provided safety and security, tethered to leaning, rusting posts.

Charlie and Aurora followed their in-mask guide-maps to a lonely hub house with a wild, dead garden and a sign nailed to a post which read: *The Wasp Factory.*

"Looks lovely," said Aurora.

"I can't believe anyone actually lives here."

"Ring the warning."

Mr Cauldhame unveiled the door after the second buzz. He was a fat, bald man with an expression somewhere between confused and bemused. He stood awkwardly, on thin bowed legs, like a frog, and was wearing a yellow jersey so tight they could see the colour and shape of the old-fashioned tie he was wearing underneath. "Yes?" he asked, his voice thick with phlegm. There was an invisible air-screen between he and the children.

Aurora began rambling but as soon as she mentioned Mr Byron, the old man waved them inside and sealed up the main door so quickly it nearly took Charlie's arm off.

The children followed him down a steep moving staircase and they all walked down to a sunroom, which, on one entire wall, had a screen showing a view from the back of the house. Sam and Aurora were stunned by the sight of a green garden full of flowers and a gorgeous blue sky outside.

"Sit here long enough and you'll convince yourself it's real," Mr Cauldhame said, putting both hands behind his back and pushing his stomach even further out. "Nice to meet you both, anyway. Nice to meet anyone these days. Byron did warn me you were coming. Have a seat, have a seat. The cushions will scoot in to hug your body, don't worry. They're set for my fat bottom but they'll adjust themselves nicely if you give them a moment."

Aurora glanced about the underground room. Charlie was mumbling something about the project. She couldn't help noticing there were lots of pictures on the walls of empty fields and forests – all old fashioned: the skies blue, the rivers brown, the fields green. There were no faces in any of the pictures which struck Aurora as strange. She had hardly ever seen images without faces. And these weren't pretty views of lovely scenes, either, they were boring images of empty countryside where there should have been people.

"I must ask you both for your favourite reads," Mr Cauldhame said, sitting forwards. He was – the children both noticed – very, very old. He spat slightly as he spoke and his eyes seemed to operate separately from his body. His clothes smelled odd, as though he wore the same thing every day, and his teeth were his own, stubbly and brown. If it wasn't for his warm, glowing eyes he would have been terrifying.

Aurora named hers – the second in a new romance series she was enjoying. Mr Cauldhame scribbled the name – *by hand*, Aurora noticed. Nobody, *but nobody* wrote by hand anymore. It was considered bad for your health. Pointless.

"And yours, boy?" Mr Cauldhame asked Charlie.

Charlie shook his head. "I don't know, always changes."

"Name one."

"I don't know. *Flowers of the Ancient World?*"

"*Flowers of the Ancient World?*" Both Mr Cauldhame and Aurora looked confused.

"Yes." Charlie shrugged. He pointed to the window. "I've never really seen flowers. Not their real colours, in the wild like that. Mum had a copy. The flowers smelled and moved and everything. They smelled really nice but Mum said they smelled nicer in real life." He shrugged his shoulders. "I used to read it every day."

"Why are all your picture frames empty, sir?" Aurora asked.

"What's that?" Mr Cauldhame cupped a liver-spotted hand to his hairy, pink ear.

"I'm sorry, sir, it's just that I couldn't help noticing that all of your picture frames are empty. They look like they should have people in them." Aurora pointed at the wall and Charlie saw what she was talking about.

"Oh, really? That's what you think, is it?" Mr Cauldhame held his eyes open a moment and shook his jowls. "We happen to think they're perfect as they are. Remind us of what we miss."

"I miss my dad," Aurora said. This silenced the room and she looked up, seemingly surprised she'd said anything.

"You must do," said a voice from the doorway. The children looked around and saw a lady with grey, tied-back hair hanging down her back, drying her hands. She was wearing a long, old-fashioned dress which reached her ankles.

"Leana, my love," Mr Cauldhame said, pointing. "These are the little ones Byron sent."

"Nice to meet you," Leana said, coming in to sit close to the others. She had piercing blue eyes and a white smile. "It's very nice to have you both here. We don't get many visitors these days."

"Sorry if this is an intrusion," Aurora said. "It's just that we're doing a project. About the history of the school. About legends."

Mr Cauldhame slapped his thin thigh and bellowed. He laughed so long and hard it ended with a coughing fit. "Ah-ha! So that's what we've become! Legends!"

"No, sir! No, not at all. Mr Byron was only saying, sir, that you might know something we could use in our project? Something about the school? The history of the school? You were the Head Boy at St Francis' once, weren't you?"

"I was, I was. Many moons ago." Saying this – the word "moon" – Mr Cauldhame stood up gingerly and staggered forward to the window. He placed his big, spotted hands on the screen. "Where is it? Where is it, then?"

"Sit down, Sam," Leana said, standing and guiding her husband back to his seat. "Come on. Don't get excited."

"When did you first come to the school, sir?"

"What's that?" the old man asked. He looked at his wife: "What's she saying?"

"Call him Sam," Leana told the children. "He's Sam, I'm Leana. Easier."

Aurora repeated her question.

"Me? What? Come here? Oh. Oh, when I was about twelve or thirteen, I think. Older than you, I suppose. My father was an archaeologist. Went to places that were dangerous. Too dangerous for a child. And my mother wasn't well." The old man drifted off again. Sometimes he wondered if he'd got something of his mother's illness: her problems. Wasn't all that had happened to him some kind of illness? Had it ever happened? Illness could be so convincing. You convinced yourself of things sometimes – made up stories in your head that you believed. These days he always said the wrong word. Said things he didn't want to say. Saw things he didn't want to see.

Charlie interrupted, nudging him as Leana prompted: "What was the school like when you arrived, Sam?"

"Oh, it was all a whole new world to me, as I'm sure it is to everyone who comes these days. Everything was new. It was like a world within a world – probably it still is."

"You can say that again," Charlie said.

Leana touched his arm. "Are you not from around here, then, young man?"

"No. I'm from... well, I was born on Mars, more or less. On the Fourth."

"Oh, my goodness. That's some journey!"

"I lived most of my life on the big Space Stations that orbit the planet. Sometimes in the New Lunar Colonies."

"Why the Space Stations?" asked Sam Cauldhame.

"Because of the storms on the Fourth," Charlie said. "Too dangerous."

"We heard it's very bad there at the moment," Leana said. "Would that be right?"

"It is. That's why we're here."

Leana pointed from Charlie to Aurora. "You're brother and sister, are you?"

"No!" laughed Aurora.

"No, my sister is Alice. Alice Vonnegut."

"Vonnegut," repeated the old man. "You're Athy's family then, are you?"

"Yes," Charlie nodded. "I'm Aunt Athy's great-nephew."

"Which means your grandmother is Kizzie Jull-Costa?" old Sam asked, suddenly very lucid.

"That's right."

"She was a Writer," Sam whispered loudly to his wife in an aside they all heard. Aurora looked at Charlie but Charlie looked back, confused.

"How's your Aunt Athy holding up with all the trouble they're going through over there at the school?" Leana asked. "I hope she's not suffering too much."

"Actually, we don't know where she is."

"Oh, no." Leana looked genuinely worried. "What do you mean?"

Charlie was about to lie, as he had been doing since he and Alice had been caught by the mods the night before, but something about Sam and Leana and the odd, charged, atmosphere in the room made him change tack. "Something strange happened to her."

"Not anything bad, I hope," Leana said.

Sam Cauldhame was leaning forwards in his chair, stroking his fat, pink double chin. His sixth sense was roused. Perhaps there was one last adventure in store for him after all. It had been so long. So very long. "Where is she? What 'strange thing' are you talking about?"

"I think she's in a picture," Charlie said.

Aurora's eyes widened. "What?"

"A picture?"

"Yes, sir. Sam, I mean. In a painting."

Sam looked at Leana, who was looking right back at him. "When did this happen?"

"Yesterday. After Assembly. After Mrs Mallowan's funeral."

"Why do you think she's in a painting?" Leana asked.

"I don't know anything about this," Aurora said, holding her hands up.

"I saw her," Charlie replied. "We saw her, Alice and me." These two, he was thinking, Sam and Leana, had the same strange way of behaving as his mother did: an interest in things nobody else had an interest in. A willingness to believe things nobody else would even consider.

"Where is this picture she's in?" Sam asked, clearing his throat.

"Upstairs in the Main Building, outside – I think it was the old Headmaster or Headmistress' study."

"Upstairs in the Main Building?" Leana repeated.

"Yes."

"In a bronze frame?" Sam asked.

"Yes, I think so."

"*Vercingetorix Throws Down His Arms at the Feet of Julius Caesar*," Sam said, nodding at his wife.

"Isn't it ancient history?" Charlie asked. "I thought it was the Romans."

"Very good," Sam replied, looking at the boy with genuine admiration. "It shows the victory of Julius Caesar over the Gauls. Gaul is what's called New France these days."

"You believe him?" Aurora asked Sam, with a look of horror.

"Oh, quite, quite," Sam replied. "And, young man. Any idea how your great-aunt managed to get herself into the painting?"

"I think it was with this," Charlie said, taking out what he'd found the night before on the floor, when the mod had caught he and Alice. A brooch and chain.

Mr Cauldhame turned the tinkling metal over in his hands and clicked the latch on the brooch. "Where did you get this, lad?"

"We found both of them on the floor by the painting. But the main bit, the brooch you're holding, we brought down from home. Mum gave it to us. Aunt Athy had the chain on when we met her. Our grandmother – er, Kizzie, we call her Granny Red – wanted Aunty Athy to have it."

Sam had found the hidden message on the back of the picture of the *Mona Lisa*. "Ah! Here we go. Yes, yes. This is Kizzie's writing!"

"Granny Red wrote it," Charlie said, nodding. "I told you."

Sam passed the brooch and chain to Leana. He nodded at Aurora. "And you were saying the Moon is very large at the moment, weren't you, my dear?"

Aurora nodded, wide-eyed. "Yes. It's enormous."

The old man raised an eyebrow. "Full, is it?"

"Yes." Charlie looked at Leana, who was looking at her husband. "Why? What does that have to do with anything?"

"It means that your great-aunt is safe," Leana replied.

"I don't understand any of this," Aurora said quietly. She stood up at a bleeping from the helmet she'd left on the floor by the doorway.

"Well, you said you were looking for a project about old legends," Sam said to her. "Now you've got one. You've got a real, live one."

"Charlie, we have to go," Aurora said.

"What's up?"

"We've been recalled."

"Now?"

"Go," Leana said. "Don't get yourselves into any trouble on our part."

Aurora was reading the message on the inner screen. "They're saying there's been a robbery at the school," she said. "We have to go back. Everyone is confined to their dorm-pods."

Charlie picked up his safety helmet. "We'll be back," he said to Sam and Leana as they all stood at the bottom of the staircase.

"Here," Leana said, passing him the brooch and chain.

"Thank you."

"No," Aurora said. She let her visor dissolve so she could talk. "If there's been a robbery, it's better to leave that here, don't you think? They'll search us at the gates as we go back in and they'll take it. There'll be guards and mods everywhere."

"She's right," nodded Sam.

"Will you keep it safe?" Charlie asked, looking at Leana.

"Of course."

"Another warning," Aurora reported, touching her ear. "We're going to get into trouble if we don't leave now."

Leana accompanied the children upstairs and let them out through the main seal. When she came back down, her husband had unblocked the windows and they could see the real view: the great brown-yellow sky and the smudged white shapes of the two children walking away towards the school.

Sam pointed at the enormous Moon. "It is full. The girl was right."

"Of course it's full," Leana replied, serious. "It wouldn't have worked if the Moon wasn't full, would it?"

"You know what this means, my love?" He let the brooch dangle from his hand on the chain. "You know what we could do with this? Right now?"

Leana shook her head. "We can't, Sam. This has been given to those children for something, some reason. Their mother gave it to them, you heard the boy."

Sam pointed at the empty pictures on the wall. "We could go back, Leana. Be young again. Together. Blue skies. Green fields."

"We've had our time, Sam. And it wasn't bad, was it? It still isn't so bad."

Sam looked out at the Moon. He clasped the brooch tightly in his hand.

XVIII

Mr Banks peered up at the pea-green rain which was beginning to splatter against the roof of the Dome. Each droplet seemed to explode as it crashed into the curved panels, leaving dark, dribbling bullet-holes.

That is not a good sign, he thought to himself, before turning back to his class.

"What's going on, sir?" a girl asked.

"It's a smog shower," Mr Banks said, trying to control his voice. Like all the other teachers, especially the humans, he was nervous. They'd all heard rumours that the new Headmaster Mr Chor-Zor had decided to do away with human teachers altogether but Mr Banks didn't really believe it could happen. *Surely not?*

"What's a smog shower, sir?"

"It's a type of rain. Come on, now, get back to your work." Mr Banks' artificial eye whirred open and closed. He didn't know whether to focus up on the green splatters or down to what was happening on the floor of the dome.

"No, Rimbo," Alice was saying. She was in a group with Roald and a cyborg called Rimbo who was having trouble understanding what they were supposed to be doing. "The idea is that we have to find out if a memory the subject thinks is real, is actually real."

"But why wouldn't it be?" Rimbo looked like a normal student but for its blank almond eyes and shiny plastic skin.

"Because sometimes we think we remember things," Alice started. She waved a hand and looked across at Roald.

"We confuse memories with things people tell us," Roald said.

"We think something happened," Alice went on. "But sometimes we remember what we want to have happened." She wrinkled her nose. "We make up the past. It's something our brain does. A survival instinct."

Rimbo cocked his head, his neck whirring. "That doesn't make sense."

"Rimbo, perhaps you could join Burlane at this table," Mr Banks said, interjecting. He'd overheard the conversation. "Burlane is reviewing the technical specifications of the new Nanos."

"Yes, sir," nodded the cyborg. He bowed politely to Alice and Roald and left.

"As you were," Mr Banks said, walk-whirring on.

"They shouldn't be trying to teach cyborgs this type of thing," Alice whispered. "It doesn't make sense to them. They don't do any of this in the NLCs or on the Fourth. Everything is separated otherwise we just all hold each other back."

"Mrs Mallowan wanted everyone to have the same education," Roald replied, also quietly. "It was one of her principles."

"But that's just nonsense," Alice replied, fighting to keep her voice down. "We're different. Cyborgs can't do experiments like this. They can't understand how the brain can't be perfect."

"Why can't they learn?" Roald looked offended. "It sounds totally unfair to separate them."

"But we're different, Roald! Cyborgs are logical, not intuitive. They can't think for themselves. If you ask a cyborg to build you a box, you have to specify everything – the sizes, the dimensions, everything, otherwise you never know what they might do. They might destroy this dome to build the box. They may try to build the biggest box ever seen and end up destroying the school, using all the materials. You have to give them limits."

"Oh, you're exaggerating."

"Maybe, but it's possible. How would they know when to stop otherwise? They can't think for themselves! They don't have common sense, no reason."

"But they have to learn! We're not in the modern ages now,

Alice."

Alice pointed at the pink brain hologram circling in front of their faces. "That is the most amazing computer ever invented, Roald, and it took millions of years to develop and we have it inside our heads. The cyborgs and mods are learning quickly but despite all its mistakes and strange ways, they'll never have anything as powerful as this for," she tried to think of a time, "years and years."

"I still think it's wrong. To separate beings. It's dangerous ground."

Alice rolled her eyes. As she did so a pain shot through her temples. "Ow."

Roald sensed the pain. "What's wrong."

"Nothing. A headache. I didn't sleep last night."

"Why not?"

"Oh, you know. What I was telling you about. My great-aunt."

"They still haven't found her?"

"No."

Roald took a sly look about the classroom. Mr Banks was standing at the white fizzing edge of the room with his hands behind his back, nervously tapping his foot. Beyond him, green streams of rain were pouring down the outside of the dome walls.

Roald said: "I actually think that's good, Alice."

"Why?"

"Because it means she's got out of here. That she's all right."

Alice looked up at Roald. She hadn't told him about the brooch and chain, or Charlie's meeting with Sam and Leana. She certainly hadn't told him about the painting they thought they'd seen Aunty Athy in. "Surely she'd die if she was outside?"

"Not necessarily."

Roald began to whisper his story: the first time he'd told anyone.

He'd lived out there, outside the domes and tunnels, he said. He'd been born on the outside, in the middle of the Great Black Sea, on Big Plastic Island. He'd grown up there but the only thing he'd wanted to do was escape. As soon as he was old enough, he'd taken any work he could get – with dome builders, pilots, medics and especially with the salvagers who'd come to search for treasure under the plastic.

"There's whole cities down there, under the Black Sea," he said. He told her how a cyborg he'd met on one diving trip had taken him back to a dome city on Safe Land and a Nano technology company it'd worked for. Thanks to the cyborg, Roald had got a job. That company was now paying Roald's tuition fees at St Francis. He'd got in here because of that and because Mrs Mallowan was his grandmother. "One day that's what I'll be," he finished. "A real Nano Engineer."

"And you'll be good at it," Alice said.

"I'll do it to make my nan proud too."

Alice put out her hand. "I'm sorry about what happened. I think it's terrible."

Roald, shrugging her off, replied coldly. "I don't want to talk about it. It's finished."

Alice stared at Roald as the boy went back to studying the floating brain. Sometimes you got so wrapped up in your own life and your own story that you forgot other people had their own lives, their own struggles and their own stories. It made sense now, Alice thought, studying Roald's bowed head, why he was like he was. Concentrated on his work, determined.

"Are you going to live there then?" Alice asked. "When you finish here?"

"Where?"

"At the company. In – where was it?"

"Safe Land? Probably. For a while."

"And then what?"

Roald's eyes darted away. "I've got plans."

"What plans?"

"You're going to think they're stupid."

"No, I won't."

Roald leant down low to the table and spoke quietly. "Ever since I was little I've had a dream. The same dream, over and over. It's blue – everything is blue, like they say the world was once – the seas, the planet, the sky. A Seer once told me it was because, in another life, I lived on the Earth when it was still alive, but I don't believe her."

"Why not?"

"Because I think it's my future. Something I'm going to see. It's like a light that draws me. Whenever I'm sad or happy. I go to sleep and I see it. Sometimes not for weeks or months but then I see it again. Like it's calling me. A blue paradise."

"It sounds amazing."

"It's all I've seen since my grandmother died. Sometimes I see her, at night. She talks to me, like a ghost, I suppose. She tells me she'll see me there."

"Who separated these cyborg children from the others?"

The voice had come from the perimeter of the room. Everyone turned and saw Mr Chor-Zor, cape flowing behind his body, face dark but for his emerald eyes and silver-studded mouth standing behind Rimbo and Burlane's desk.

"I did," said Mr Banks, straightening up.

"What you have done, sir, is very grave and strictly against protocol."

"I can explain," Mr Banks said.

"You will explain in my office," Chor-Zor replied. Two modifieds with blank faces, in dark gowns, stepped through the invisible classroom wall and raised stun weapons.

"Please come with us. You will be subdued if you struggle."

As Mr Banks stepped up to the guards, they flanked him and some kind of energy charge attached them to the teacher by his wrists. This must have been painful because Mr Banks closed his eyes and his throat contracted although the children heard no sound. He was quickly marched out through the wall, feet hardly touching the ground.

"Mr Pull-Mun will take over this class until further notice," Chor-Zor said and everyone watched as Pull-Mun, wearing a grey cape, and with his face set in a steely frown, stepped through the wall.

"Enough theory," were Pull-Mun's first words. He made a sweep of his gloved hand and every floating pink brain in the room disappeared. "From now on, as protocol dictates, we will have only practical work in the labs."

"Vonnegut," Mr Chor-Zor declared, pointing at Alice.

Alice lifted her head. "Yes, sir."

"You will come with me. Now!"

XIX

The bad news travelled quickly, racing down the tunnels and reaching the Kwad just as Charlie and Aurora were finishing explaining to Mr Byron what had happened during their strange visit to Sam and Leana's house.

"All the human teachers are being rounded up, sir," cried a breathless boy skidding in through the doorway of Mr Byron's room. "Seriously! You have to get out of here!"

"I beg your pardon?"

A girl pushed forwards from behind the boy. She had red hair, freckles and wide-open blue eyes. "It's true, sir! The mods are replacing all the human teachers. They're taking them away."

Mr Byron turned to Charlie and Aurora and tried to concentrate on what they'd been talking about. "Well it looks like we haven't got time to beat around the bush so I'm going to be straight with you. If Mr Cauldhame and the legends of the school are to be believed, some kind of magic is afoot which connects the disappearance of your aunt and the full Moon. I believe that's what Sam was making reference to."

"But how, sir?"

Mr Byron's eyes flickered to the doorway. "Oh, that's not for me to say. That's not for me to say. One believes in these things or one doesn't. I've certainly had cause to doubt scientific explanations – but the truth is, I don't know what's going on in this instance. Perhaps now is not a bad time to believe in miracles."

The first boy had been looking down the corridor. He turned with panic writ on his face. "They're coming, sir!"

"Hide, sir!"

"Where's the brooch now?" Mr Byron, visibly pale, asked as he backed away. The children came over and huddled together around him, all backing away from the dark doorway, protecting him.

"We left the brooch and chain with Sam and Leana, sir," Charlie said.

Aurora explained, speaking quickly: "We guessed there were going to be checks at the main gates. We didn't want them to find them and take them off us."

"Do you still have your passes?" Mr Byron asked them, brightening slightly even as his eyes flickered nervously between them and the doorway.

Charlie nodded. "Yes."

"Then go! That's what you must do. Go back to Sam and Leana's and get the brooch. Ask them what to do – they'll know. They'll know better than anyone." Mr Byron widened his eyes and shook his arms at them. "Do it now, both of you – it looks like there's not much time. Say I sent you, if you get asked." Mr Byron shrugged. "It looks as though I'm in trouble anyway."

Charlie looked at across at Aurora. "What do you think?"

"Are you sure, sir?"

"I'm not sure about anything," came the resigned reply. "But it looks like staying here and doing nothing is a recipe for disaster."

"Why don't you try and escape too, sir?" Aurora said. Some of the other children nodded. The redhead in the doorway waved at him. "They've gone into one of the other classrooms, sir. You've got a chance. Make a run for it!"

Mr Byron looked down at the children around him. "Do you really think so?" Without answering, they pushed him towards the doorway, where he turned and clasped his hands together. "You are good children – all of you. Remember – no fear, no envy, no meanness!" And with that Mr Byron and his silent monkey turned on his heel and swished away.

"Now what?" someone asked.

"Shall we go?" Aurora asked Charlie.

Charlie was thinking about his answer when the crowd of

children in the doorway drew aside and the dark figure of Mr Chor-Zor appeared with an equally blank-faced Row-Lin right behind, like his shadow. She had taken on the same grim aspect as Chor-Zor and Pull-Mun but her fake hair was as long and sleek as ever. There were swirls of scarlet and silver patterns flowing from her eyebrows on to the patch of skin between her eyes and hair.

Chor-Zor beckoned for the children to sit down, on the floor or chairs, and scanned the room. Row-Lin had gone straight up to Mr Byron's desk and was tapping at the departed teacher's screens.

"Where is he?" Chor-Zor asked the class. He didn't need to name names.

The students remained mute.

"Very well. As Mr Byron seems to have deserted you, I am here to announce that from now on you will have the very good fortune of having Ms Row-Lin as your tutor. Nothing else will change. You will remain in this classroom, following the new protocols."

"No sign," Row-Lin stated, coming over to stand front and centre with Chor-Zor. "He left all his tags here." A steely smile formed on her face. "Seems he left in a hurry."

"Another one runs away like a coward," Chor-Zor answered.

Charlie put up his hand. "Please, sir."

"Yes, Vonnegut?"

"We know where he is, sir."

"*We?*" asked Chor-Zor, taking a step forward. All eyes were on Charlie. Some of the children had gasped in horror at the betrayal.

"Aurora and I, sir," Charlie answered. He smiled nervously into Aurora's terrified-looking gaze.

"Pray tell, Vonnegut."

"It's not easy, sir. I'm not sure how to explain it. It's a place only he knows. We were there with him a while ago, sir. A secret place off one of the tunnels, near the back gate."

Chor-Zor cocked his head. "A secret place? Do you have the location?"

"No." Charlie shrugged. "That's what he said, sir – that it was secret. Not on any screens or maps. He only let me take him halfway and Aurora had to take him the rest of the way. That's how both of us know. She knows how to get halfway there and I know how to get the rest of the way."

Chor-Zor looked puzzled. "But where exactly is it, Vonnegut?"

Charlie shrugged. "Not far, sir. About three-quarters of the way down the tunnel which leads to the back gate. Down that way, sir, from the Kwad. I haven't been here that long, sir, I'm not sure of all the names."

A longer pause. Another mod arrived, cowled in black, and relayed whispered information to Chor-Zor. He turned back to Charlie and swished his glove. "Go then, both of you, and find him. Quick as you like!"

"Yes, sir!"

"Track them," Chor-Zor told Row-Lin as Charlie and Aurora ran out. The Headmaster shouted after them: "If you're not back in four and a half minutes you will be followed, collected and severely reprimanded."

"Four and half minutes?" Charlie shouted, running backwards down the corridor, setting a timer. "Right, sir! Thank you, sir!"

He ran behind Aurora as they hurried down the stairs to the deep tunnel which led out of the Kwad. Only when they were on their own did Aurora slow down, turn and begin to shout at him: "What do you think you're doing, Charlie Vonnegut? Are you insane?"

"We had to get out somehow! You heard Byron!"

"That was Mr Chor-Zor there! Do you know what they are going to do to us in," she looked at the time in the corner of her eye, "three and a half minutes?"

"No. What?"

"I don't know! Kill us?"

"They can only kill us if they find us," Charlie replied, leading them both further down the corridor. "And who cares, then, anyway? If they find us, we've failed."

"Charlie!" Aurora laughed. "Of course they're going to find us! Oh, I don't know why I even let you get me into this?"

"You're doing this because you know what's really going on!"

"What's going on? The only thing that I've seen going on is that the mods have taken over the school and they're angry with everyone, especially humans. And what are we doing? Well, we're lying to them and running away from them!"

"You want to do what they say?"

"I want to live, Charlie!"

They stopped at a small side-tunnel which both of them knew led to the village exit gates. Charlie stopped and put his hands on Aurora's shoulders. "Come on. We have to do this."

Aurora took a deep breath. "When life is boring you kind of wish for adventure but when you get one all you want is your boring life back again. Have you ever noticed that?"

"I promise you'll get your boring life back again," Charlie said. "Just come on, will you. They're going to know as soon as we turn down here where we're going."

"But I do want an adventure," Aurora was saying, more to herself than anything. "I do. I want adventures. I really do."

"Tell me something you want. Something you want to do when all this is over. Anything."

"I want to see my dad," Aurora said, eyes wide in her mask. But she blinked and got angry quickly. "Oh, but that's stupid, impossible. What are you making me say? Why are you doing this, Charlie? It's not funny, messing with people's emotions like this."

"I promise you'll see your father," Charlie shot back.

"Don't! Don't say stupid things."

"Aurora, look at me." He waited. "I promise you'll see your

father. And soon. We'll get out of here. Trust me, if I want to something, I do it. I don't want to be here anymore than you. I don't know how, but I will get you – us – out of here. I'll make sure you see your father again." He softened his grip on her shoulders. "I wouldn't mind seeing Jjohn's City again."

Aurora, who was very serious, suddenly broke into a smile. "Oh, you're such a... I don't know what you are."

"Can we go now?"

"Go!"

They ran up the earthen-walled tunnel to where the protection suits were hanging on hooks on the wall.

"And if there's a guard out there?" Aurora asked, slipping into the sleeves. "Like before?"

"We'll say we've been sent back by Byron. He said he'd back us up."

"Where do you think he went?" Aurora asked quietly. "To hide?"

"Somewhere safe, I hope."

The children gave each other the thumbs up and Aurora zapped open the door lock. They walked through into the middle capsule, sealed both doors, equalised the pressure and unhinged the gatelock to the outside world. The gloopy yellow-cold day came in to meet them – they could feel it like cold sludge against their suits – and as they stepped out on to dead earth a single drop of green rain exploded in the middle of Charlie's visor. "Oh, man!" He thought he'd been shot. As he wiped the thick drop it smeared across his screen, pea-green.

"Yuck! Is that stuff toxic?" Aurora asked.

Charlie said he had no idea. "Let's just get to Sam and Leana's house. Quickly."

Mercifully there were no guards outside the school and they walked out into the deserted village unmolested. Both knew, although neither said it, that they must have been approaching the time limit Chor-Zor had mentioned: no doubt they were also being tracked. Mods would be after them shortly. Then they would be – what was it? Followed, collected and severely reprimanded.

"Time's up," Aurora noted. There was a sad little bleep from somewhere in her visor. "Let's hope Sam and Leana know what to do."

"Save your air."

But as they approached the Cauldhames' home – in single file, careful with the debris and rocks – Aurora heard Charlie cry out. She thought he'd been wounded. "What's up? What happened?"

"Look at the house."

Aurora stepped alongside Charlie and saw dark smoke billowing from the windows and doors of Sam and Leana's home.

XX

Alice was marched along the corridor by two blank-faced mods in capes and gowns. Mr Chor-Zor had left them at the intersection for the Kwad without saying another word to her. Students and teachers, horror in their eyes, parted as the three made their way towards the main building.

Alice felt nervous but also angry. She was angry because she thought what Chor-Zor and the others were doing was wrong. She was also worried about Aunt Athy and what they'd done to Mrs Mallowan, and hated that the mods seemed to think they could do whatever they liked to anyone whenever they wanted. But she also knew that they did have the power and that everyone was scared of them – she could see it in the way everyone moved out of their way in the tunnels – and she knew that she was so emotional she would probably burst into tears if she got into an argument with anyone.

The only thing she could do, she realised, was stay calm and see what they wanted to do with her.

In the Main Hall the mods spoke between each other.

"Where do we take her?"

"You don't know?"

"I wasn't given orders."

"Me neither."

"Ask."

"You ask."

"I am a Mark 2. Protocol dictates you ask."

"Accepted. Stay here. I will ask."

One mod went back towards the tunnel and Alice stood beside the other in the weak light of the entrance hall. It seemed a long time since they'd arrived there on the *Giraffe* and had been met by their aunt. Alice looked up the old wooden stairs and thought of Romulus and Remus: she must go up there and feed them. The idea of cleaning the flat made her feel nauseous.

As she looked about Alice saw she and the mod were not alone – an elderly couple, someone's parents or grandparents, were sitting in one corner of the hall near the large empty fireplace, arguing. The man was fat and bald, and the woman had long, grey hair.

"Oh, you're so stubborn!" the woman cried out, standing and walking away towards Alice and the mod. She spoke with an accent Alice didn't recognise. Alice thought she might perhaps be from one of the mining moons.

"*I'm* stubborn?" called out the man. It took him a great effort to stand. He came over on bandy legs to where Alice and the mod were. The lady had gone right across to the other side of the hall and was standing pretending to read the wall which had the names of all the Head Boys and Head Girls of the school. She was tapping her foot.

"Excuse me," the man said. He had a very fat, pink double chin and looked supremely unhealthy. "My wife seems to think there is a meeting of the Magistrate here today."

Alice didn't know what to say. She shook her head as if to say: *Don't ask me. I can't say anything.*

"No meeting today, sir," said the mod.

"Oh, aye, there is!" the lady piped up. "In the Eleusinian Room." She'd obviously been listening.

The man wobbled his neck. "Yes, yes, I know it's in the Eleusinian Room but there isn't one of those here anymore, is there, my dear? If you could get that into your head we might be able to get somewhere instead of going around in circles!"

"The Eleusinian Room is nearby, sir," said the mod.

"I beg your pardon?"

The mod, programmed to answer politely, elucidated: "The Eleusinian Room is just around the corner there, sir. Take note that restricted access is in operation."

"Just around that corner there?" asked the lady, coming

across to the group.

"Around the corner, ma'am," agreed the mod.

"Where?"

The mod looked at Alice. "My duties do not permit me to show you. This girl is to be punished. Protocol dictates she is accompanied at all times."

"I'll accompany her!" The old man grabbed Alice roughly by the elbow. "Go, will you. Just show her where the room is so she'll shut up once and for all about this meeting!"

The mod computed. "Very well."

He and the old woman walked away and immediately Alice, who was bewildered, heard the old man whisper in her ear: "Take this brooch, Alice. Your brother Charlie gave it to us. My name is Sam Cauldhame and I know what's happening to you. There's magic in the brooch. Twice more before the full Moon wanes you will have the opportunity to go into works of art. Take the chain with you if you wish to get back out of the picture. That's how your Aunt Athy escaped. She's in the picture upstairs where you found this and I'm quite sure she's safe. She doesn't want to come back – we think she wants you to go to her."

Alice turned to the old man. "H-H-How do you know all this?"

"Oh. That's another story."

They both turned as the old lady – Leana – and the mod came walking back.

"Well?" Sam asked roughly.

"I don't understand it at all," the old lady said.

"No meeting," said the mod.

"I told you!" Sam shouted, leading Leana towards the front door. "I told you but you wouldn't have it!"

Alice heard the second mod returning. "The girl is to be taken to the lower dome cells," he reported, clumping over to them.

"Cells? What for?" Alice asked, the brooch and chain gripped tightly in her hand.

"Questioning," replied the mod. "This way please."

XXI

At the tunnel crossroads, Alice and her two mods met Mr Banks, also accompanied by two guards. Alice smiled at the teacher's familiar face but neither of them spoke. The mods swapped information by holding up their palms and formed a circle around Alice and Mr Banks as they shuttled them through a restricted passageway and then down a series of staircases to the lower dome.

"Which room?" asked a mod.

"Drop Banks in the hold first."

Drop Banks in the hold. The phrase chilled both Alice and Mr Banks as they were prodded onwards.

The lower dome seemed to be a series of bare steel staircases and shadowy areas filled with humming pipes and grinding machinery. There was much cold concrete, barely lit, and, but for the odd puddle or scuttling rat, it seemed quite empty.

"May I ask what is going on here?" tried the teacher.

"No you may not."

Two floors further down, along a clanking passageway, they came to a halt outside a thick steel door in the wall. When this was opened, Alice and Mr Banks were faced with the sight of twenty familiar faces, all teachers, all humans, huddled together in a dripping cell. Although the walls were modern and shining, if dirty, the ceiling was sagging, green in places, and dripping what was hopefully water. It was brown and gloopy, and the humans were huddled together in the dry patches, trying to avoid the spreading puddles the leaks had caused.

"Mr Banks, please step forwards," said one of the mods.

"What is this?" he asked.

"A holding cell. Step forwards. You will be attended to in time."

A black-iron robot with a humanoid face stepped out to meet

them. "Identify," it said, holding up a fingerless hand.

One of the mods held up their own hand and a series of silver flashes passed between them.

"Enter, Banks," the guard robot said.

Alice was ordered to move on and did so, helpless. She heard the thick door close behind her and tried not to think about what she'd just seen. So that was what they were doing. That was Chor-Zor's plan. There was no doubt about it now.

As they walked on the corridors became lighter, straighter and more modern. Alice had the feeling they were walking in a very long semicircle. When they finally stopped, it was in front of a fizzing white wall.

"Reveal," a mod guard said.

A bare, also fizzing room appeared and Alice was told to step inside and await further orders. There were two boys, both young, kneeling and playing with a transformer machine inside the room. They glanced up at her but went back to their game.

"Hi," Alice said. She was glad to see someone – anyone – there. When she looked back, the door had rematerialised. The room was a cube of shining white. The ceiling went up very high to a small very black square at the top. "What are you guys doing?"

"Transmodelling," answered one, not looking up.

The boys were placing objects into the front bay of the machine and then commanding it to change the molecular structure of the object. Most of their requests were rejected with an angry buzzing sound but sometimes the machine was able to do what they wanted and the pencil or tie or shoe which they'd put in came out as a marble, a sock or a cup. When this happened they clapped and high-fived each other.

"Ms Vonnegut," came a voice from beside her. Alice looked up to see Chor-Zor. Where had he appeared from? "Come with me, please."

"Yes, sir."

She followed the Headmaster through a dark rectangle which

had formed in the wall and they found themselves alone. This was a small cell with standard walls but Alice could hear the air ventilation system somewhere above them, the same system she'd heard during the school assembly. From this she deduced they were somewhere close to the dome: they had indeed walked in a circle. Perhaps they were right underneath it?

"I'll keep this brief, Vonnegut. It's bad news, I'm afraid."

"What is it, sir?"

"Well, it seems that your great-aunt, before she ran away, stole an article of school property. Not a very valuable article. A superstitious item, decoration, really – an antique – but she stole it nevertheless. Protocol dictates that she is now to be considered *persona non grata* at St Francis' and that her misdeed is to be reported to the local security forces."

"What did she steal, sir?"

"A book."

"Just a book, sir?"

"Yes. An old-fashioned book. A sentimental item, made of thinned wood."

"But why is that so...?"

"She stole property that wasn't hers, Ms Vonnegut, and I should remind you that this means that as her kith and kin, both your brother and yourself will, if your aunt does not reappear to face charges in the next twenty-four hours, be liable for the theft."

"But that's not fair!"

"My advice to you, young lady, is to find out where your aunt is. Until we realised The Book was missing, we did harbour doubts as to what might have happened to her. However, now I and the entire Magistrate are convinced that your aunt's disappearance and crime were premeditated. This was all planned in advance."

"But then where is she?"

"That is for you and your brother to find out. And to find out quickly."

"But where's Charlie?" Alice asked. "I haven't seen him since Assembly."

"He's in the main Sick Bay in the dome," Chor-Zor replied, reading the information off his internal screens.

"Sick Bay?"

"He was Out of Bounds without permission, accompanied by a girl. His suit was deactivated and he breathed fresh air."

Alice covered her face with her hands. "Oh, that's terrible. Is he all right?" When she took her hands away she was alone. "Mr Chor-Zor?"

A door shot upwards revealing the empty corridor and a hologram of an arrow, pink and purple, flashed in mid-air, indicating which way she should go.

Vacate ante-room in five, four, three, two…

Alice stepped out and began walking in the direction shown, thinking about Charlie and what they were going to do. What she really wanted to do was leave all this behind and go back to her family on Mars, especially as it sounded like they were also in danger. Yes, it was dangerous there and yes, there were storms, but anything was better than being here. The only thing wrong with just leaving, though, was that if they left, they would also leave their great-aunt behind. Their mother would never forgive them and they would never forgive themselves.

No, they had to stay. They had to sort this out and then go home. Which meant Alice needed to go see Charlie in Sick Bay. There was no option.

Alice stood a moment staring down the long, empty corridor, not realising she'd taken a wrong turn and had walked away from the arrows. Nobody was tracking her because no mod would ever believe anybody could take the wrong direction when there were enormous pink arrows flashing in the air to show the way. But Alice *had* taken a wrong turn and now she was here, walking down old service corridors, not sure which way she was going.

As she was about to turn back she thought she heard something, like clanging, someone banging a hammer against steel perhaps, and the growling whoosh of fire guns, from the far end of the corridor she was walking along.

When she got right down to the corner, Alice saw she'd been right. There were people working – she saw hammers and fire guns – but what caught her attention was the enormity of the space she was looking at, and what was in it. She was standing in the corner of a kind of underground hangar – a huge, airy, high-ceilinged space with a great space cruiser hovering in the centre. The ship was sleek and silver, and various platforms and metal scaffolds had been set up around it: various workers were firing and hammering at the sides.

"Can I help?" a young cyborg asked, lifting off one of his ear-protectors as he squinted at her. He had been made to look like a human, a year or two older than Alice, and he had dark stains on his cheeks which were supposed to look like dirt. She knew he was a cyborg because of the double pupils in his eyes. "Have you been sent down to work with us?"

"No," replied Alice, honestly.

"You're not on Ship Engineering?"

"No." She pointed at the cruiser. "What is that thing?"

"This is the school's inter-system ship. Four-year project, world government funded. *The Mallowan*."

"Inter-system?" Alice knew what that meant: the silver cruiser in the middle of the hangar was designed to travel between solar systems. There would be life-pods inside. People would grow up and die aboard the ship. She had seen one on the Moon, an old one, but this was the most modern version she had ever seen. "Is it secret?"

"What? No! Every school has one! Inter-Governmental policy. Nobody knows what's going to happen these days. You saw the storm the other day, right?"

"Everyone has them?"

"Everyone has them. Security measure. If you ask me, it's a good thing. Course it means they've given up on ever saving the Earth but I say it's better to head on upwards instead of sitting here till the bitter end anyway."

"But how far along is it? Is it operational?"

"What's going on here?"

Alice and the boy turned to see another cyborg, this one in a dark mask and blue overalls, coming over on four bronze legs.

"I thought she'd been sent down to help," the first said.

"I was looking for the dome," Alice replied.

"You've come the wrong way," said the cyborg. "You're out of bounds. Go back up the S-3. Keep going to the junction with S-4 and follow the pink arrows."

"Ah, the *pink* arrows," Alice said, shaking her head. "Not the blue ones, the pink ones. Great, thanks."

"Blue arrows?" asked the youngster, scratching his head.

"Get a move on," the cyborg barked. "And you," he added, tapping the other. "Back to work. What do you think you are? Human?"

XXII

Alice was amazed at how much the dome had changed. Not physically, for it was as huge and imposing as ever, but the atmosphere inside.

Where before it had been such a bright, cheery, noisy place, the only sound now came from the tinkling of the false fountains and the tweeting of the fake birds. The pupils moved about in silence, gliding up to the higher rooms and classroom spaces like sleepwalkers. Groups of mods stared out from raised platforms, sensors hanging from their shoulders like dark wings. Alice had seen such contraptions before: they were to allow the mods to monitor everything and everybody without having to move.

Alice walked under a hologram banner hanging over the main space which said:

**ALL
TOWARDS
PERFECTION**

In the classrooms there were no human teachers, only mods. The human 'look' also seemed to have suddenly gone out of fashion. The mods all had plain faces – no human features, only clear skin. Some had dots or shining points of light for eyes, some moving lines for mouths, but all the lips, noses, chins, freckles and wrinkles had gone.

As she passed out of the dome, heading for the Main Building, and came to the Sick Bay stairs she was confronted by a mod she had never seen before, blank faced, with a pale grey cape – the lightest colour she'd yet seen.

"Can I help you?"

Even their voices, Alice thought, were now neutral. Not male or female. Like Charlie before, these small changes didn't bother Alice as she'd seen most of this on the Mars ships and on the Moon. There mods had developed their own cultures. "I'm looking for my brother Charlie Vonnegut," Alice said. "I was told to see him by the Headmaster."

"He's downstairs in Bay One. Use the lift. You'll need to be scanned."

Alice did as she was told, standing in the fizzing white space and watching the red scanner line rise from her feet – closing her eyes, as she must, as it passed up over her face – before she descended quickly to the lower level. An arrow began flashing the moment the door dissolved and she followed it, to another door with a plaque next to it which read SB1-CV. Alice guessed CV was Charlie Vonnegut and, after a warning bleep, she came face to face with Aurora.

"Oh, Alice! It's so good to see you! Come in."

"How is he?"

"Annoying," replied Aurora. The girls walked together into the small room where Charlie was lying on a bed with belts over his chest, knees and ankles. "He's supposed to stay still for three more minutes and then we can go."

"Alice, get me out of these!" Charlie shouted.

Alice looked at Aurora. "Three more minutes?"

"Three more minutes and we can go. They said it. He was quite badly poisoned. We went Out of Bounds and they switched us off. It was terrible." She touched Alice's arm. "Your brother saved me, really. He let me use his air, what was left. He breathed the outside air."

"Charlie," Alice said, walking over to the bed which was suspended in the air in the middle of the room. "What have you done? Look at you."

"Alice, please get me out of here. I've been in these straps for five hours. They've tied me down, given me injections, prodded me – I don't know."

"Aurora said three more minutes and we can get out of here."

"They said that before." Charlie squirmed and the belts stretched. An alarm sounded until he lay still. The clock on the roof reset to three minutes and began counting down. "Ah! I hate this!"

"Did they say it before?" Alice asked Aurora.

"Yes, but because he was struggling so much they had to give him more lung cleaner. I saw the readings, Alice. They weren't lying."

Alice was worried but she touched Charlie's forehead. "Please just wait three minutes, Charlie. I'll stay. If they don't let you out this time, I'll deal with them."

"We have to get out of here!" Charlie cried through gritted teeth. "You don't know what's going on. We went to see an old Head Boy from here and he told us everything. We know where Aunt Athy is!"

Alice's eyes widened. "Where?"

"In that picture."

"What? Which picture?"

"The one upstairs: the Julius Caesar one! Where we found the brooch and chain." Charlie shouted out in frustration and banged his head back on to the hard bench. "Ah! And we were supposed to get the stuff back from Sam and Leana but the mods got to them first. Burnt their house."

"I think I might have met them," Alice said. "An old man and woman were in the main hall. They gave me this." She held up the brooch and chain.

For the first time since she'd arrived, Charlie lay still. "Wow! Where did you say you got that?"

"I told you. An old man and woman who were in the hall in the main building gave them to me."

"Sam," whispered Charlie, smiling.

"And Leana," added Aurora. She came over, crouching to look at the twirling brooch: "Alice, as crazy as this sounds, that thing has some kind of spell on it, some kind of magic."

Charlie nodded. "Sam told us the spell, or whatever it is, will work three times while there's a full Moon. And there's a full Moon right now. Aunt Athy obviously used it once, so that means there are two goes left."

"Two goes what?" Alice asked.

"To go into the picture."

"You're not seriously suggesting that we should go into the picture too, are you?"

"Yes. That's what Aunt Athy wanted. Think about it."

"Oh, this is too crazy," Aurora said, walking away, hand on her forehead.

"Wait! Aurora. Perhaps it's not so crazy," Alice caught the other girl by the elbow. "It actually makes sense that Aunty Athy planned all this. I know it sounds weird, but I think she just might be in the picture. Hiding. Chor-Zor just told me she stole something from the school. A book. Perhaps she took it there with her. Perhaps that's why she went."

"You've been with Chor-Zor?" Aurora asked, eyes wide. Since they'd been brought in to Sick Bay she'd been terrified of what was going to happen to them. Before Alice came in, she and Charlie had been trying to work out what they would say when they were inevitably questioned.

"Seriously, Aurora, Charlie, it's terrible what they're doing," Alice said, holding the other girl, looking at her brother. "They're rounding up all the human teachers and have them downstairs in a horrible cell, all crushed in together. Mr Banks is there. I saw Mr Byron too. It's in the lower dome."

"Why?" asked Aurora, horrified. She looked at Charlie. "They caught Mr Byron!"

"I don't know. I don't know." Alice shook her head. "It's awful."

"This doesn't change anything," Charlie said. "We have to find Aunty Athy. Alice, one of us has to go into the painting and find her. There's nothing else we can do. We know she's in there.

She left the brooch behind on the floor. I think she wanted us to go in there too."

"But why?"

"Probably because it's safer in there than here," Aurora said, and nodded as they both looked at her. "Let's face it, if she was here, she'd be down there in that cell with all the others, wouldn't she?"

Alice looked at her brother. "Do you really want to try and go into the picture?"

Charlie nodded. "Definitely."

Alice shrugged. "I don't know. I guess we have to do something, though."

"I need to speak to Aunt Athy," Charlie said calmly. "She'll know what's going on. I know she'll know what's going on. I can feel it."

"You really believe she's in a painting?" Aurora asked.

"We saw her," Alice said.

"If she's not – if it doesn't work – then we'll think of something else," Charlie said. "But we have to try. Let's go up there, do whatever we have to do and see what happens!"

As the girls remained silent, thinking, a bleeping sound was followed by three clipping noises and the belts holding Charlie in place popped open.

Congratulations! You are cured! Patient SB1-CV, please make your way back to the Kwad! Follow the flashing arrows. Be perfect!

"Let's go," said Charlie, sitting up and rubbing his wrists. He swung his legs about, stretched, and jumped off the table. "Come on."

They went back upstairs in the elevator and walked out into the dome as calmly as they could. Nobody challenged them as some classes had been let out for lunch and the space was busy with crossing children. Now Aurora and Charlie noticed what Alice had seen before. People were scared. There was an iciness to the atmosphere, a cold, detached feeling which hadn't been there before. They saw the uniforms, the guards, the new faces.

At the tunnel to the Kwad, they stepped out of the busy flow of children. "You two don't have to come upstairs with me," Charlie said. "It might be better if I go up alone."

"I'm coming," Alice said. "I've got to get the brooch, remember. You can't go in with it."

"I'm coming too," Aurora said. She looked at Charlie, not sure what to say. "You made a promise, remember?"

Charlie nodded. "Of course I remember."

"We're coming," Alice said. "Let's go. Keep moving."

"You're both crazy."

They took the short tunnel to the Main Building – the sky bruised and bright yellow – and came up through the empty doors into the familiar-smelling old entrance hall. "They'll turn this into a museum or sell it off," Charlie said as they headed for the stairs. "Worth a fortune all this old stuff now."

"This is where I saw the old couple. Sam and Leana?" Alice said.

"Where did they go?" asked Aurora.

"I didn't see."

Aurora pulled a worried face. "I hope they got away."

Charlie led the way up the creaking staircase. There was no way of avoiding making a sound. When they came to the landing with the threadbare lime-green rug, Charlie pointed his own key torch down into the shadows and sighed with relief. "The painting's still there. Come on."

Alice touched Aurora's shoulder. Aurora had stopped on the landing. "What's up?"

"I heard something. The door downstairs, I think. Maybe they followed us?"

"Charlie," Alice whispered as loudly as she could. Her brother was almost at the painting. "Do it! If you're going to do it, just do it. Someone's coming."

Alice heard noises too – creaking on the stairs. The noise

seemed to come from upstairs, not down. "Come on, let's just make sure he goes." She walked quickly backwards down the carpeted corridor. Aurora followed, catching up alongside Alice, turning back to look at the dark doorway to the staircase for any intruders.

Charlie stood in front of the painting. *Vercingetorix Throws Down His Arms at the Feet of Julius Caesar*: it said so in tiny writing at the bottom of the bronze frame, why hadn't he noticed that before? This was it. He looked to where they'd seen the woman who looked like Aunt Athy before. "She's not there," Charlie whispered.

"What?" Alice craned her neck, breathing loudly. It was true. "Oh, no. You're right. She's not."

"Here!" Aurora cried, unable to control her voice. She was pointing at another place in the painting, the grey smudge of a crowd in front of the burning castle. "That's her, isn't it?"

"Oh, wow, yes, I think so," Charlie answered, squinting. He couldn't see properly in the weak torchlight. "Are you sure, Aurora?"

"Not really," Aurora answered. She heard a loud creak behind. "Oh! They're coming! They're here. Get a move on!"

"Go," Alice told her brother. "*Go!*"

The creaking became louder – there was more than one person coming.

Alice heard a thud behind herself and turned, ready to hiss at Charlie again but Charlie was gone.

Aurora screamed – she had seen bright eyes in the darkness, glowing eyes coming. Alice scanned the painting quickly. No sign of Charlie. She looked down and saw the brooch and chain on the carpet.

Aurora screamed as Romulus and Remus came bounding into the torchlight.

XXIII

Chor-Zor was in the office they called the Cockpit. It had been built under the highest part of the dome and was suspended, hanging by a narrow demodulation tube, the only exit and entrance, from the roof structure. Through the floor he could see the tops of the trees and waterfall and, much further down, like ants, the students and teachers crossing the floor.

The Headmaster was reviewing the situation, trying to work out how many new modified students they would need to bring in to keep the school profitable when they finally phased out humans. Second on his list of worries was a name for the school. St Francis was an obscure saint from an old, obsolete religion: the school needed a new name to reflect the new direction he planned to take it in.

Finally, he needed to work out what he was going to do with the humans he was starting to accumulate down in the cells. All the human teachers had now been rounded up, and he knew it was a matter of time until he sent out the order for the human students to also be herded up and sent away. The question on his mind was: when to do what he knew he had to do? What he knew must happen. Just as Ma'am Mallowan had been removed, so must humans from St Francis'. The question was, to act or wait and let nature take its course?

"Headmaster?"

Chor-Zor looked up and his features formed. "Speak."

"You have a visitor, sire."

"Who is it?"

"Deputy Head Row-Lin, sire."

"Urgency?"

"High, sire."

"Very well. Tell the DH to descend."

Chor-Zor stood near the smoke forming in the centre of the

XXIII

room. Row-Lin appeared slowly, her molecules reforming from being separated in the tube, kneeling.

"Stand," ordered Chor-Zor.

"Head-of-School, sire," Row-Lin began. Interestingly, she had kept her feminine voice, Chor-Zor noticed. He liked it. Perhaps he would leave the room voice as it was. Row-Lin remained bowed, composing herself. While walking across from the dome she'd thought she'd seen Ma'am Mallowan standing at the crossroads of two empty tunnels. It had obviously been a trick of the light, some small problem with her memory banks, but it had made her nervous and unsure of herself.

"Well? What is it? What do you want?"

"I have a recording, sire." Row-Lin lifted her gloved hand and a recording began to play. It was from Sick Bay. "I think you will find it interesting."

"Who's that?" Chor-Zor asked. "Vonnegut, is it?"

"Yes."

"When? The last I heard, they were caught out of bounds. That little liar said he knew where Byron was. I sent him out after him but he was trying to escape."

"That's his sister visiting," Row-Lin replied, nodding, highlighting Alice. "The other girl is Aurora Morpugo."

"Yes, I see. Where is this?"

"SB-1."

"When?"

"Four and a half minutes ago, sire." Row-Lin might have smiled if she'd been human. "I think you might find their conversation very interesting, sire."

The flickering image of Charlie in Row-Lin's palm shouted: *Get me out of here!*

Chor-Zor watched the scene play out with mounting interest.

137

XXIV

22 August, 55 BCE
Old England

The little green man,
the little green man –
just as she said –
the little green man.

There he goes,
earth for his bed,
leaves as pillows,
clouds for his hair!

Just as she said!
Little green man –
Oh, please come back!
Little green man!

Charlie could hear the whispered song.

The cold damp air roused him. It was the first time in his life he'd ever tasted real air: it was sweet and delicious and you felt it rush all the way down your throat and fill your lungs with life and greenness until you were lifted up on tiptoes.

Looking up, he saw the high, dark treetops swaying against a lighter sky: the leaves swished and waved at him, changing colour subtly. It was dying night, perhaps dusk or dawn. The whispering came again, a swish-swash of sound, leaves against leaves but a voice too. Pattering rain sprinkled from somewhere up above, not quite reaching where Charlie was, lying on his back among high ferns and long, green stalks of grass.

Little green man, came the voice again.

Charlie leapt up on to his haunches: he was in a clearing in a forest. The high leaves flashed and shuddered like silent, warning hands.

"Who's there? Who is it?"

My God! The fresh air was exhilarating! He felt alive to his sopping toes. But he was terrified, too – peering into the deep green shadows between the encircling boughs for the source of the voice. There were birds tweeting birds, leaves pattering and, as he moved, twigs crinkled and cracked under his weight.

Thick forest spread out in every direction. Charlie saw a toad, throat filling, croak burping out as he watched. An owl hooted – so owllike and perfect it had to be real. Or were the animals signalling? Was this a feelie? What was he supposed to notice?

Little green man! Just as she said!

This time the voice was more insistent. Determined. And Charlie placed it: a very dark patch of shadow in front of a huge spotted elm trunk. He saw eyes, too: human eyes.

"Who are you? I can see you! Step forwards!"

"Little green man!"

The strangest boy Charlie had ever seen came out of the shadows with a sharpened, flint-tipped spear poking the air ahead of him. The boy was wearing animal skins and a hood which might have been a bear's head. His skin was badly marked, the whole left side of his face sloped like melted wax. His eyeballs were two very different colours, one dark blue, the other pale, almost perfectly white, and he walked hunched over, like an animal, a wounded monkey, one knuckle on the ground. "Little green man! Little green man! Oh, she said you'd come here, little green man!"

Charlie looked about for something to defend himself with.

Seeing this the other boy held up a hand. "No, no, little green man. Oh, no, no! I mean you no harm!"

Charlie crouched, fists up, ready to fight. "Who are you?"

The boy was turning his singular face, examining Charlie,

smiling in wonder at the lack of eyebrows, at Charlie's large, almond-shaped head. "Oh, little man, pray tell – did it hurt, when you fell from the stars?"

Charlie cocked an eyebrow. "What?"

Both of them turned at a fierce howl from the woods close to the clearing and the boy in the bearskins backed into the shadows he'd come from, beckoning Charlie to follow him. "Come hither, little green man, or be meat for the curs!"

Charlie didn't need asking twice. He'd never been more frightened by a noise than by that roar, and every instinct in his body was to move very quickly in the opposite direction. He followed the wild boy into the undergrowth, tucking his hands into his sleeves to avoid his skin catching on the sharp thorns he suddenly noticed. The ground beneath his feet was springy. Charlie saw the Moon high above, full but distant. Unmarked. Tiny, like Phobos looked from Mars.

"Dem beasts are hungry at night," the boy was saying, giggling. He moved quickly and skilfully through the forest on feet and knuckles, occasionally tugging or directing Charlie. "Dem eat, eat-eat all what roams at night – little pink men, little green men. Hehehe."

Charlie looked nervously over his shoulder and saw their path marked by pressed down ferns but nothing else. The darkness was so deep back there it seemed to fizz.

"Down!"

The boy held Charlie and they crouched together. Before he could do anything about it, the boy pinched Charlie's lips closed with his dirty fingers, signalling for him to keep quiet.

"All right," said Charlie, pushing the boy's hand away. The boy smelled, frankly, disgusting: he'd obviously not washed in a long time and his hair had a reeking, cheesy smell which made Charlie, now that they were at such close quarters, gag.

The boy bowed his head and Charlie stared at the head of the bear the boy was wearing over his upper body. It was a real bear but for the eyes. The eyes were a kind of stone or pebble but the fur looked real. It smelled foul, too, like a live animal: waste, dirt and excrement.

"What are you doing?" Charlie asked.

"Beast coming," the boy said, his breath foul, making a play with his black fingernails on his hands. He'd attached something to his boots and stood up as quietly as he could. To Charlie's horror he took off the bearskin and passed it across. "Shroud yourself, little green man."

"Oh, no."

"You smell like food!"

"All right, all right." Somewhere he knew what was going on. There was some kind of wild animal after them and the boy was worried Charlie's smell was going to give them away. He could see the sense in that. But it didn't make it any easier to put on the skin coat, especially when he saw the interior was fleshy pink and looked clammy. It smelled putrid.

The boy kicked his toes into the bottom of the tree trunk they were standing beside. "Rachlan climb. You stay."

So your name is Rachlan, Charlie thought. He held his breath and covered himself with the skin.

The boy went up the trunk with tip-tack digging noises.

Down on the forest floor, Charlie listened to the pattering of the rain and looked out at the dark ferns and grey trunks. Raindrops dolloped off dock leaves. Gradually Charlie became aware of a sound like a purring. It was a throaty purr, perhaps the beginning of a growl. And it was coming from just where those two yellow eyes were forming in the darkness dead ahead.

It's some kind of cat, Charlie thought, surprisingly calm. *A big, wild cat.*

There was little he could do. Run, perhaps, but his legs felt like jelly encased in lead. He thought about Alice. Perhaps this was all a dream? He thought about his mother and father. Where were they now?

The cat, lithe and brown, stepped out of its hiding place and slinked towards him. It was a beautiful creature, bearded, with short ears and big fangs. It watched Charlie closely, licking its lips, and this licking, this obvious sign of its intentions, finally set the boy off. Charlie bolted and at the same time the cat sprang, claws flashing out like knives, but before it landed it yelped in pain as Rachlan fell upon its back with his homemade spear, lancing it quickly and painlessly into the next world.

Charlie had run with his eyes closed for ten metres before tripping. He was lying on the ground, eyes and teeth clenched shut, poised to be eaten. Instead of the cat's screams, though, he heard Rachlan's voice. "Wake up, little green man. Move on, move on. More beasts hungry tonight in the night."

Charlie didn't need asking twice. He even helped Rachlan tie up and drag the corpse of his would-be attacker, and they made quite a pair: the hunchbacked boy with his bloody spear on his back and Charlie, in his bearskin, pulling a rope apiece, flattening the ferns and nettles dragging the body of the lynx.

After what seemed a very long trudge, Charlie caught the whiff of smoke, of a fire. His friend beside him was smiling and made a sign as if to say, "not far now, not far now." They came to the bank of a river, toffee-coloured and fast moving, crossed it on a wooden bridge and followed what soon became a pathway. There were large stones along its borders.

Not long later the river widened and Charlie became aware there were people coming out from among the trees clad in skins. They had long hair and Charlie thought they were mostly men, though it was hard to tell. Rachlan was talking all the time and these inquisitive, slightly wild-looking humans smiled at Charlie, raised their hands and made gestures with their eyebrows which Charlie recognised as welcoming.

"Little green man," Rachlan was telling everyone proudly.

Some of the men came over and examined the lynx. One hoisted it up on to his shoulders and used it to scare a group of dirty-faced children who were standing in a confused huddle further down the path.

Soon they were entering some kind of village and dogs were yapping at their ankles. Rachlan was obviously proud of Charlie, and Charlie felt relieved more than scared at what he saw. The people's eyes were friendly and welcoming. Charlie noticed ducks and pigs and children kicking something between themselves behind a big roundhouse which had smoke puffing from a central chimney spout. Much bigger than all the other buildings in the village, Charlie hoped they were going to go inside but, instead, they passed by and walked out through the other side of the village, back into the woods.

"Where are we going?"

"Walk, walk."

Charlie was confused but did what was expected of him, following Rachlan uphill along a steep but well-marked path. Alongside them rose a steep, slate cliff, high, rocky and green on its ledges. Down below, down steep, leafy hills, he could see the winding brown river.

After a long climb, and feeling quite exhausted, Charlie looked up to see a large mousehole-shaped cave opening in the rock cliff dead ahead of them. Groups of hairy, dirty people were sitting outside around campfires and some stood as Rachlan whistled. The men, women and children came down to stare and greet them but Rachlan led Charlie through them to the mouth of the cave, which was much bigger and more jagged than it had looked from the path. Just as he was wondering what was going on, he heard his name and a familiar voice.

"Aunt Athy!" Charlie cried, seeing his aunt, dressed all in white, standing in the doorway of the cave.

"Come in, come in, Charlie," his aunt said. "I thought you were never going to come. Step inside then." As he went to hug her she wrinkled her nose. "Oh my, oh my! What on earth are you wearing?"

XXV

New England
The future

Alice and Aurora half-jumped, half-ran down the stairs, coming down into the entrance hall just as they heard a barked command from the tunnel entrance around the corner, out of sight. "Let's check upstairs first," a mod voice said.

"They're coming," Alice whispered. "Where shall we go? Back upstairs? Maybe we can hide in Aunt Athy's place?"

"No! That was disgusting!" They'd taken Romulus and Remus back to Athy's flat, which had been filthy and untouched. Aurora tapped Alice's arm. "Over there – the main entrance. We'll go outside. They'll never come after us."

Alice looked across to the door. It was where they'd come in the first day: it seemed like years ago. "Are you sure? How?"

Aurora was dragging Alice. She could hear the mods coming into the hall. "There are protection suits by the door. They leave them for visitors. Come on."

"Ah, yes! I remember! They were hanging up!"

Aurora led the way. They ran across, squeezed into the safe-lock area and Aurora resealed the door to the hall as quietly and quickly as she could. Now they were alone with the beige day they could see beyond the clear protective screen. "There," said Aurora, pointing at the helmets and suits in a cubbyhole. "Come on, let's put them on."

Alice turned back to the door. "Are you sure this is a good idea?"

"No, but what do you want to do? Go back in there with them? If the mods find us they'll want to know where Charlie is. We'll be prisoners."

"Maybe they aren't looking for us?"

"Oh, yeah. Sure. They're probably here looking for the cats."

Alice put on her mask. It smelled of bad breath and the mouthpiece tasted old and stale. "Oh, this is disgusting."

"Lock into me," Aurora said, pointing at the settings on Alice's sleeve. "You're on public now. Everyone can hear you. Change it."

Alice did so. "Can you hear me now?"

"Yes." Aurora nodded. "Are you secure? No leaks?"

Alice read her controls. "I'm fine. Not much air, though."

"Me neither. But let's go."

"Where are we going?"

Aurora pulled a face. "Anywhere. Let's try and find another way in to the school. We need to stay out of the mods' way until Charlie gets back."

Alice agreed – what else could they do? She took the lead, stepping through the screen and felt the weight of the brown atmosphere on her legs and feet immediately.

The black, spiky trees surrounding the front lawn seemed curiously alive: this was an effect of the thick, woozy, moving air. Behind the jagged boughs hung the low, full Moon. It was enormous, yellow and mottled like fresh cheese. Aurora couldn't help looking up and thinking of her father. How long did he have left? She also thought of Charlie's promise to take her there. It was sweet of him, but people shouldn't make promises they couldn't keep. She felt a flash of anger. Weakness. Hope.

The two girls followed a path along the façade of the old main building and Alice turned to look up to admire it – it was like a red-brick ghost house, turrets poking up into the sooty sky. Perhaps in better weather this would look like the old pictures of the school she'd seen. Her mother had shown her wonderful presentations about St Francis': ah, the thought of her mother! It came with a feeling that gripped hold of Alice's heart and squeezed it, hurting her physically. How she missed her! Her father too. How much she would love to be with them, bundled up in their love.

"Keep an eye on where you're going, Alice," Aurora warned her. "If you trip or snag something you'll spring a leak and that'll be the end of both of us."

"Can the mods come out here?" Alice asked, looking back. There seemed to be nobody else outside; nothing moving but the gravy air. It was like being at the bottom of a dirty, murky pond.

"Not without asking for orders," Aurora answered, a smile in her voice. "They'll need to go back and get suits, too. That's if they even know we came out here."

"Phew. That's something then." Alice remembered the cupboard upstairs, where she and Charlie had hidden once. There had been suits in there. Maybe that was where the mods were going?

"In any case, those two we heard won't come out. They'll send lower types or cyborgs and that'll take even more time."

"That would all be great if we actually knew where we were going."

"True."

The girls picked their way quickly but carefully through the ruins of the old school buildings. Almost all the classrooms and living areas were underground now but once upon a time this had been the main area of the school. Some of the old buildings still stood: ghostly houses, abandoned, shells without windows or doors. Alice was staring into one of them – an old boarding house – when she thought she saw a pale face – a scary head. "Oh!"

"What is it?"

"I thought I just saw someone. Over there. In that building."

"Yes, it was probably an abjad."

"An abjad?"

"Was it a weird white-green thing?"

"Yes. A face, I think. Wrinkled. Horrible!"

"Definitely an abjad. They're the only ones who can live on

the surface. They've adapted. They have special lungs."

"And they live here? In the buildings? Seriously?"

"They live everywhere." Aurora seemed more concerned with picking out a route through the fallen leaves, potholes and stones. "The mods think they're vermin but that's only because the abjads suck the energy out of mods if they get hold of them out here."

"*What*?"

"Haha. About the only thing abjads don't eat are humans. Some people say they used to be humans – they're like a race of humans. Relatives. You probably just saw your uncle! Haha."

"So they're not dangerous?"

"Not for us. Not unless you're a mod or a cyborg."

Alice could hear her own breathing loud and raspy in the helmet. The air was starting to run out and her lungs hurt – squeezing, sticking together, chest tightening. "How much longer, Aurora? Do you know where we're going?"

"Not long. Come down here. Follow me."

They were walking down a debris-strewn path with the dome rising on their left, a lovely, mercury-coloured bubble. It was impossible to see inside from out but its form and design – its scale – was very impressive. Alice noticed a strange ruined space on their right, cracked black concrete strewn with markings and tattered nets and posts. It was something she recognised from books and films her parents had shown her. "Oh, wow. Is that where people used to play outdoor sports?"

"That's right. Ages ago."

"Tennis!" Alice said brightly, happy she'd remembered the name. "Look! Some of the nets are still there."

"If you touch them they turn straight to dust," Aurora replied. "If you stand on any of that place, it just crumbles, dissolves. It's totally unsafe."

They were walking downhill now, through sooty, charred plants, beside an empty shell of a building. "I've got another question, Aurora. That's just reminded me."

"What?"

"Our ship when we came down here was called the *Giraffe*. I saw some of the other Earth ships in the NLCs were called *Elephant* and *Whale* and things like that. Are they all named after animals? That's what those names are, aren't they?"

"They're named after *extinct* animals," Aurora replied.

"Oh." Alice was going to go on and explain how, on Mars, the ships were named after exoplanets but it was getting hard to speak. "My air is really getting low," she said, her voice quiet. "I'm starting to feel dizzy."

"Then stop talking and save your breath." Aurora pointed at a mound among the scorched grass on the other side of the ruined sports area. "There. See that? That little hill? It's an old airlock entrance. Hardly anyone uses it anymore. Some of the classrooms collapsed down here and they moved everyone up to the Kwad. I just hope the old codes still work."

Alice looked back over her shoulder at the dome and the Moon. There seemed to be no sun, but it must have been somewhere behind the fug of cloud. The sky was glaring. On the roof of the ruined building they'd just walked past she saw those odd limey-white figures again, sitting very still, watching. They looked like monkeys or gargoyles.

"Here we are," Aurora said as they got to the mound. She keyed in the code. "Oh, great. It works. Go on. You go first."

Alice looked into the darkness. "I don't like the look of it."

"I need to lock us in," Aurora said. "Go in. It's fine!"

Alice went first, stepping through the security screen and feeling her way down a set of steps. She descended clumsily, noticing from the settings on her visor that the air was still impure. "Are you there, Aurora? This is horrible. I can't see anything."

"Keep going. Down to the bottom."

Down Alice went, to a glowing light at the bottom of the

staircase. Passing this, she ducked under a low beam of tangled roots and found herself in an earth-walled chamber half-divided by a bright glass wall. Behind the glass were two interlocking green trees – sycamores – covered with flags and ribbons. Alice instantly recognised the trees – she'd been shown pictures of them at Granny Red's and her mother's, many times.

Aurora tapped her on the shoulder. "You can take off your mask in here."

"What is this place?" Alice asked, ruffing out her hair. She took a few soothing, deep lungfuls of the familiar school air.

"Nobody knows."

"I've seen it before! My great-grandma used to show it to me. Pictures of it."

Aurora was nonplussed. "People used to come here to be alone, that's all I remember. It was popular when I first came here. For some reason it has this artificial light all the time, like old sunlight. Some people say it's magic but there was a study a while back and they said it's actually a radioactive element in the leaves which creates the light. This tree is some weird mutation – a mutant tree. That's why it shines. In the end the Magistrate decided to cover it with the glass and leave it here. It's connected to the rest of the school by a tunnel. I'll show you now."

"It's beautiful."

"It's kind of beautiful if you believe in that type of thing, magic, love and all that rubbish. But once you know the science behind it, it kind of takes the magic away. People stopped coming because they think it's dangerous. I told you: radioactive. Believing in love is dangerous, Alice."

"The light moves."

"I know. They can't explain everything." Aurora pulled Alice by the elbow. "Come on, we ought to keep moving. Let's go inside and try and find somewhere to wait or hide. It's not safe here. Maybe we can get hold of a screen or some communications and find out what's going on."

Alice nodded but she couldn't take her eyes off the trees. She felt, somehow, that she was in the presence of her great-aunt, her mother too. Finally, though, she let herself be dragged into the low, dank, dripping tunnel and the girls began to run back down the tunnels towards the dome and school.

"Where does this passageway come out?" Alice asked. The way was lit by thousands of tiny pinpricks of light in the walls and ceiling.

"In the service tunnels under the dome."

"The other day," Alice began, remembering the huge hangar she'd found – where the ship had been, near the place they were keeping the human teachers.

"Sshhh!" Aurora shot out her hand and it hit Alice in the chest. "Someone's coming."

"What?"

"Sshhh!"

The two girls looked ahead. Minuscule beams of light from the dot holes in the walls criss-crossed each other and they both heard a noise: feet stamping. A figure appeared at the next corner of the tunnel. "Alice? Aurora?"

Alice's fear turned to a kind of nervous joy. "Roald?"

Roald came running down to them. "Oh, am I glad to see you."

"How did you find us?" asked Aurora, stunned.

"Tags on the suits," said Roald. "Everyone's tracked you, it's all over the coms! I saw where you came in. Well, I guessed from your route. I just hoped I'd get here before anyone else. Looks like I did." He smiled at Alice. "What happened to Charlie?"

"Gone." Alice held up her hands. "Don't ask. He's fine. Just don't ask."

"Oh-kay." Roald pointed back up the tunnel. "You guys have to get out of here. They're looking for you. And Charlie. And me too now, I guess."

Aurora asked: "What shall we do? Go back to the Kwad?"

"Impossible," Roald replied. "They've started rounding up the human students. They used you guys as an excuse."

"What?" Alice looked horrified. "What are they doing with them?"

"Same thing as the teachers," Roald replied. "Holding cells, under the dome. It's not pretty."

Aurora sighed. "We're in big trouble."

Roald shook his head. "Not really. How do you think I got here? There are ways of avoiding them." He pointed up the tunnel. "Just up there is a security door. They'll be waiting for you but," he pressed the tunnel wall and the panel flipped, revealing a tight passageway. "I have a plan B."

Aurora smiled. "Wow! Really?"

"There's food, a place to sleep, all the comforts of home in there." Roald held out his hands. "What do you think I used to do in the holidays? My grandmother was the Headmistress, remember! I used to come here and play, especially when they were building the dome. I know this place like the back of my hand."

Roald held out his hand for Alice. "Come on. Let's get going."

"No."

"What?"

"I'm not coming."

Aurora, who'd climbed in already, turned and peered out of the hole. "What? Alice, come on! This is our only chance. We hide out, think of what to do, wait for Charlie in here. You heard what Roald said, if we go through that security lock we'll be put in the cells with everyone else."

"I can track everything from in here," Roald agreed, pointing to the tunnel. "You're not going to be much use to Charlie or your aunt in a cell under the dome, Alice. Plus," he narrowed his eyes. "I wasn't going to tell you this, but there are other people in there. Villagers, hiding. The mods gutted their houses."

"No, no." Alice put her fingers on either side of her temples, trying to concentrate on a crazy thought which was forming. "I know it seems like the right thing to do but I have another idea."

"What?" asked Roald.

"Wait. I'm thinking." She looked at Roald, eyes bright and fierce. "You said they've been tracking us? They knew where we were, right?"

"Yep."

"How?"

Roald shook his head but thought about it. "They had the grab from Sick Bay. I heard them talking about that."

Alice nodded again. Now she was smiling. "I think I know what to do."

"Oh no," Roald said. "What's going on? What's that weird look for?"

"Nothing. You two go in there. Stay there. You said you can follow everything from in there, right?"

Roald nodded. "Uh-huh."

"Right. One thing: how can I talk to you?"

"Suits. Any protective suits, especially the school ones. Change the tags to public if you want me to hear you. I can follow you anywhere but if you want to talk, do that. Put the speakers on."

Alice gripped Roald's hands. "Right. Then trust me. And keep listening."

"Alice," Aurora said, at the mouth of the hole. "Are you sure this is what you want to do?"

Alice nodded. "Stay safe and be ready, Aurora."

"For what?"

Alice winked. "For a little bit more adventure."

Aurora shook her head. "Oh, I can see you're Charlie's sister."

"Be safe, both of you."

"We'll be watching you," Roald said, climbing into the hole.

"You make the signal, we'll be there for you. Wherever it is."

"Go." Alice helped them with the panel.

"See you on the other side," said Roald, sealing Aurora and himself in from the inside.

Alice turned and ran uphill towards the sealed security door.

XXVI

Old England
The past

Charlie awoke to the sound of the village cockerels crowing.

Snake-eyes blinked out of the embers, the ground was cold but he was warm under his pile of rugs. He stretched, yawning, amazed again at the taste and effect of pure, fresh, real air. Behind him were several other mounds, some snoring, some shuffling. Dawn had broken and the sky was salmon pink. Looking out through the cave entrance Charlie could see the burning sun creeping up over the high, green, treelined hills.

Crawling out of bed Charlie took a stick from the fire and poked the flames and embers. He walked over to the cave wall with the black twig, not really thinking about what he was doing, only of where he was, of how strange this place was – and how wonderful it was too – looking out again at the breaking dawn. In many ways being there, in the past, or in the picture, or wherever he was, seemed more real than being at school. Mars had been real – being down there on the surface, visiting the volcanoes, flying over Olympus Mons and skating on the ice-caps – but this was something else.

Last night the villagers had all been so friendly to him that he felt part of this place already. He'd only spoken to Aunt Athy for a while: she'd been happy to see him but had seemed worried about what was happening at the school. She'd asked him about Alice and Roald and Aurora, but had gone to bed early. Charlie had sat up late into the night listening to stories and songs with the villagers.

Ah, and that smell of trees and grass! The taste of fresh, running water! Animals! Birds! Fire!

"What are you doing, Charlie?"

Charlie turned around and saw his great-aunt. "Oh, hi, Aunt

Athy. This? I don't know. Nothing. Why?"

"What's that you've done?" Athy placed a hand on the wall next to the shapes Charlie had drawn with the burnt end of the stick. "That's something, not nothing. Do you know what this is?"

"Just some patterns Granny Red taught me."

"Granny Red?" Athy smiled at the mention of her sister Kizzie. "Ah, of course. Of course it was her. Of course she showed you this. Of course she did."

Charlie looked at his doodles on the cave wall and wrinkled his nose. "I don't think it actually means anything."

"You don't know what it is, do you?"

Charlie wrinkled his nose again. "No. Are they pictures?"

"No. It's writing."

Charlie stuck in his chin. "Writing? What, like letters? Coms?"

"No, Charlie. Handwriting."

"What's 'handwriting'?"

"It's the old way of doing what you do now with your eyes or machines."

"Using, what? Your hands? But why?"

Aunt Athy smiled and pointed at the letters Charlie had written. "Because that's how we did it before machines and your eyes wrote for you."

Charlie had noticed the floorbound shapes stirring in the cave interior. The fires and youngest children were being fed. Sunlight crept down the rock tunnel, illuminating the crevasses and stalactites, warming all, gently waking the villagers.

"Writing is how you pass ideas from people to people," Aunt Athy said. "Generation to generation. People once wrote in books. Books are collections of ideas, of wisdom, of hopes and dreams. Of what people think."

"Like databases?"

"Something similar," Athy said, nodding. "You know, this cave is full of old writing. Deep inside here there are chambers covered in writing. The oldest type of writing. Almost as old as humans."

"Where?"

Before Athy could explain they were both drawn to shouting coming from outside the cave. It was a man in skins running up to the entrance. Charlie thought the man was smiling, laughing, but quickly realised the expression on his face was terror and fear. "Invasion!" the youth was shouting, waving his arms. "Invasion!"

The word was loud – like an alarm. Dogs began yapping as the men and women around the fire stood up and more came running out from the darkness of the cave. Charlie and Athy stepped outside.

"What's this?" someone asked. "Explain yourself!"

"What's going on?"

"Invasion!" the breathless young man repeated, gasping for air. He pointed back towards the village. "Romans! Coming in over the sea. Hordes of them! We think it's Caesar."

"When? Now?"

"Right now!"

Another group of villagers came clattering up the steep path, all armed. "They're coming!" one of them yelled. "The boy does not lie! The Romans are looking for somewhere to land! Grab your weapons, all! To the coast! To the coast!"

As almost everyone set off downhill, Athy grabbed Charlie by the hand. "And where do you think you're off to, young man?"

"To fight!" Charlie replied. He tried to escape her grip but she was strong.

"What?" Athy shook her head. "No, no, no. You're not here to fight."

"Aunty Athy, please." Charlie almost shook himself free. "I have to!" He stared at her. Behind the old lady's white shoulder, the green cliff rose high over the cave entrance and was topped with great oaks. Clouds floated by in the sky, casting moving shadows. Charlie didn't know why but he felt he really did have to help the villagers. "Rachlan saved my life, Aunt Athy. I can't just do nothing: I have to help them! Please let me go."

"No. Not you! You must go back to the school."

"What?" Charlie looked downhill and saw chariots pulled by oxen and bullocks clattering away between the elm boughs. Men and women had rubbed mud or coloured chalk on their bodies and this made the whites of their eyes glow. Occasionally there would be a call and all would respond as one, shaking their spears and bows and shields.

Athy was trying to think of what to do. Seeing Charlie write on the cave wall that morning had made sense of much of what was happening. She was beginning to understand what Kizzie had wanted her to do by sending down the brooch but she didn't know what she was supposed to do with Charlie. Should she send him back to the school now? Was he supposed to fight? "Oh, Kizzie!" she said, looking upwards to the sky. At that moment Athy noticed dark clouds gathering on the horizon where the coast would be.

"Granny Red would want me to help these people, Aunty! I bet that's why she sent me! I promise I'll be careful – I'll stay out of the way."

"Be careful? Stay out of the way? That's Julius Caesar who's coming, Charlie! The man in the painting at school! This is no joke. It is a very serious matter – it's real war, not some kind of simulation!"

"They're my friends and I'm here now. How can I not help them?"

Athy looked up again at the far-off rain clouds and an idea struck her. It was a risk but it was a risk worth taking. It might be a way to – if the expression wasn't too violent – kill two birds with one stone. "Very well," she said, letting go of Charlie's hand but keeping a grip on his wrist. "You may go."

"Yes!" Charlie balled a fist and prepared to set off.

"Wait!" Athy grabbed hold of him again as he bounced on tiptoes, anxious to run, a huge smile on his face. "You can go on one condition."

"What? What?"

"One condition, Charlie, or you can't go at all!"

Charlie rolled his eyes and threw up his free hand in frustration. "Oh, you're just like Mum – what? What?"

"If, for any reason, you find yourself suddenly back at St Francis', you will do something for me."

"Fine. What?"

"You will go to my room and look under the cats' bed, under the rugs on the sofa. There is a secret cubbyhole there and in it you'll find a book, the book the mods think I stole from the school."

"Under the cats' bed?" Charlie wrinkled his nose at the thought of it. "No wonder the mods never found it."

"Exactly." Despite the gravity of what she was telling him, Athy smiled. "I need you to take out the book that you find inside it and write in it. Write exactly what you just wrote here. What your grandmother taught you."

Charlie was trying to pull away. "Fine! I will!"

"You promise? You know how?"

"With a stick?"

"With a special stick you'll also find in the hole. Look for it. A small stick which will make marks in the book."

Charlie pecked his aunt's cheek, backing away. "Yes, yes – whatever you want!"

"And find Roald and your sister and Aurora!"

Charlie was running: "I will!" he shouted at the treetops.

Athy covered her shoulders with her shawl and watched him go. She saw him run down to the bottom of the hill and run alongside the back of the cart filled with warriors, men and women. The blue-faced soldier who pulled him up on to the back of the cart passed Charlie a spear. *What would your mother say?* Athy thought. She walked into the shelter of the cave and prayed for rain.

Charlie, squeezed into the back of the cart, let them paint his face and sharpen his spear. There were slaps on the back and slaps on the side of the cart as they bounced their way out of the forest and along the ruts in the open meadows which led to the cliffs. The wind slaked them, the sky was dark grey and angry, but Charlie and the others were in good voice – there was singing and shouting and a fierce atmosphere which bonded them all together.

Charlie didn't ask himself why he felt as he did: perhaps it was something in that green, fresh air. All he knew was that he wanted to protect these people as they had protected him. And he would.

He heard stories about this Julius Caesar who was coming: about how he'd conquered Gaul. About how, as a young man, Caesar's boat had been captured by pirates and Caesar had told them that if the pirates didn't kill him he'd hunt them down and kill *them*. And how, when he had escaped, Caesar had gone after the pirates, found them and crucified them all. *He wants to be the ruler of the world,* someone said.

Aye, well not my world! answered another, to cheers.

"Be careful, lads! He's a tried and valiant soldier, not to be taken lightly," came the voice of an old hand, bearded and tucked into a juddering corner.

"Aye, so's my horse," shot back a wag – and everyone laughed.

"Here we are!"

"All out and on foot!"

When the men and women jumped out and began moving around the cart, the brisk, buffeting wind coming off the sea almost knocked Charlie horizontal. Ahead was a great panorama – the open English Channel – and, on its wind-chopped waves, were long Roman boats with billowing orange and yellow sails, filled with screaming soldiers. There must have been at least fifty vessels and thousands of soldiers.

Charlie's hair streaked out behind him. "Wow!" Alice would flip when he told her about this.

All along the clifftops around him were warriors like the villagers, some dragging large catapults and slingshots into place, others dropping stones and rocks into ammunition piles. Along the entire zigzagging length of the clifftops rode painted, hollering warriors on chariots cutting mud tracks in the billowing grass. The wide sea below was rough and cold looking. Gulls hung in the air, almost stationary, cawing, watching the scenes unfold as thunder rumbled.

"Heaven's belly is empty! It wants souls!"

"They're drawing back!"

Behind and around Charlie, thousands of javelins were rattled and voices were raised.

"They're moving down the coast!"

"Follow 'em!"

"They're going north with the tide!"

"Stay with them!"

The headland Charlie was on was narrow and ended in a bluff which dropped down sharply to the rock and pebble beach. Charlie turned and ran back to the great crush of people, beasts and carriages pouring on to the main inland road. The younger and stronger simply ran, Charlie among them.

Sometimes soldiers or villagers would appear on a stile or shout from the window of a cottage or above the hedges or fences: "They're still sailing north! Keep going! Keep going! Show 'em what for!"

When Charlie was tired he hitched a lift on a passing cart. Nobody spoke. The wheels juddered and spun in the puddles. The sky brooded but did not break. They reached another bluff, wide, windy and battered by the incoming sea gale. And there was the Roman fleet again – much closer in this time – some soldiers already disembarking in full armour, wading in through the grey waves to shore. What Charlie had thought was rain in the sky was a hail of javelins, spears and rocks from the catapults of the soldiers around him.

Charlie, fearless, followed some of the others who were scrambling down the scree and chalk of the cliffsides and, when he got down to the damp, soggy beach, heard the invading Romans' cries, loud as day. Oars were chopping the water and the metallic helmets of the soldiers glinted like their raised weapons.

"If they dare get out of those boats, make 'em regret it!" someone shouted, and Charlie walked across the sandy scree towards the waves.

There were other boys and girls, as young as he was, walking out too, spears and shields raised. Everyone was armed, ready, but Charlie felt nervous suddenly. His legs were weak. He heard nothing in his ears but a very high-pitched sound and then his own blood pumping. He felt the icy, long-running waves flop over his feet and chill them to the bone.

Curses were ringing, warnings blaring, horns howling.

Charlie turned and looked back at the high cliffs, at the hands waving in the air on the white-chalk edges, at the brooding, angry black clouds above. He looked down at the sand, at the seawater disappearing, sinking. And then, raising his spear in his frozen hands, he looked up at the Roman boats and was horrified to recognise a face.

Chor-Zor!

Dressed as a Roman soldier. Wearing the Roman uniform. A human face, yes, but those same dead, determined eyes he'd always had looking back at Charlie from under the flapping orange sail.

Pull-Mun was beside him. And Row-Lin. Both in battle armour. Both human-looking but definitely them. He could see it from their reactions. They were like salivating wolves when they saw him, all three standing, lifting their weapons, leaning over the bow of the boat to get closer to him.

Charlie was tripped by a sloshing wave. Had he fainted? Been hit? Fallen?

All went black.

All was silent.

XXVII

New England
The future
A few minutes previously

"Don't bother arguing, Alice," said Mr Banks rubbing his forehead. "They know everything."

"Listen to your teacher," Mr Chor-Zor said.

They were in Mr Banks' old classroom, the Nano machine set up and humming. Security mods were standing shoulder to shoulder in front of the invisible, fizzing walls and the dome floor, far below, was empty.

Mr Banks was thin and dishevelled. His cheeks were sunken, stubble growing over the jutting bones, and his mechanical eyes were squeaky, rusty from the humidity in the underground cell.

"Well you'll have to unlock these wrist-cuffs if you want me to do anything," Alice said. When Alice was angry her mouth became very small and pursed. "I insist Mr Banks works the controls."

"Very well," Chor-Zor agreed.

"If we are really going to do this, Headmaster," Mr Banks said, stepping forwards, "and I really cannot repeat how much I think this is a terrible, terrible idea..."

"Do stop whining." Chor-Zor didn't even look in the teacher's direction. "We're doing it and that's that."

"But, sire, Mr Chor-Zor, sir, are you sure it's a wise idea for all *three of you* to travel? I'm not sure this Nano system has ever supported more than one journey."

"Yes, I'm sure." Chor-Zor took a step forwards to where the masks were lying on the work surface. "Row-Lin, Pull-Mun and I are going. That is fixed and settled and there will be no more argument." He looked at Alice. "By the way, where is the painting your brother and aunt are hiding in with the stolen book?"

Before Alice could answer a mod in the doorway said, "Pull-Mun is bringing it, sir."

There was a horrible silence in the lab.

Alice was still and calm, angry but controlled. She had given herself up at the gate and been taken to Chor-Zor immediately. There she had watched the evidence he had shown her, of them all in Sick Bay talking about the painting, and had agreed to take part in an experiment to send the three mods into the painting with the last attempt they could make with the brooch.

Mr Banks, on the other hand, was a ball of worry. He was weak from lack of food and his eyes hurt in the bright classroom lights. Downstairs had been a horror: all the teachers crammed into one tiny underground room, the students beginning to be herded in as well. Now, being brought upstairs for this strange experiment, Mr Banks didn't know whether to be glad to be out of the dungeon or to feel guilty about what he was being asked to do.

"Ah. Refreshments." Chor-Zor nodded as a mod came over with a tray.

Mr Banks couldn't stop himself grabbing at what was on the tray but Alice shook her head and remained still. She was slightly shocked to see the way her old teacher crammed the food into his mouth, gulping for breath between bites. It told her everything she needed to know about how they were being treated in the basement and made her strengthen her resolve to do what she had to do.

"How on earth do you isolate an idea anyway?" Chor-Zor asked, amused more than interested. For a moment he seemed a sweet old man asking questions about modern technology. But Alice knew Chor-Zor was afraid of the machine: instinctive, irrational, illogical ideas were something no mod ever had or ever will have.

As she walked across to the Headmaster she knew she was in

control. This risky little idea of hers just might work. "There are particular areas of the human brain which generate ideas, sire, or, at least," Alice touched her own head, "here and here. When you are all set up we will fly down to this place in my brain and, when I look at the painting, you'll hopefully be able to catch a ride on one of the ideas that forms in my mind and enter that world."

Chor-Zor noted the change in the girl. "You seem very calm all of a sudden?"

"I just want to see my brother and aunt again, sire," Alice replied sweetly. "That's the only thing that matters to me now." She stared at Chor-Zor. "I trust you to look after them when you find them."

"Oh, we will certainly do that."

Row-Lin and Pull-Mun arrived carrying the bronze-framed painting from the corridor in the Main Building.

"Ah! Finally!" Chor-Zor sounded pleased.

"Where do you want it, sir?" asked Row-Lin.

"Anywhere in front of me, where I can see it," Alice replied. "You three should really get into your suits now. Mr Banks, have you finished eating?"

"I don't know if I have the strength for this, Alice," Mr Banks protested weakly, still chewing.

"Have another energy pill, sir," Alice replied, darting him a serious look with her eyes. "Take up the controls, please."

"Suits, Vonnegut?" asked Mr Chor-Zor. "I thought the Nanos worked perfectly with masks?"

"Well, if you want to appear to whoever is in the picture as headless figures, go right ahead," Alice replied, putting on her own mask. "I hope your brains work, too, without your spinal cords."

"Suits," ordered Mr Chor-Zor and the three mods dressed.

Mr Banks was nervy and unsure but the food and drink were working. He did feel better. And this was work – science

– something that he knew and loved. As the machines flickered into life at his fingertips, his instincts took over. "Everybody check in, please," he began, going over to Alice to check her mask and eye-pads were properly fitted. "How's your vision?"

"I need to be slightly closer," Alice said.

"Is it so important?" scoffed Row-Lin.

"Unless you want to be sent flying into the fabric of the wall," Alice replied, using the same tone of voice she'd spoken to Chor-Zor with. Alice knew Row-Lin would be nervous as well. The three of them would. And rightly so. "Yes, it is."

"Mr Chor-Zor, sir," came Mr Banks in the earpieces. "Could you check your systems, please? The red information scrolling down your left eye screen now, sir."

"All in order, thank you."

"Mr Pull-Mun, sir?"

"Also fine."

"Ms Row-Lin, ma'am?"

"All in order."

"Very well." Mr Banks was tweaking an instrument on the underside of the main machine. "Please, all of you, be aware of the position of the pale blue circle you can see hovering there at the side of your vision plates. You can't look at it, it will drift when you do, but you want this always safely in the white, all right? Try not to concentrate on it and you'll see it. Now if the purple dial you see up above goes too far down you're at risk of your suits depressurising and we don't want that. It would make an unholy mess of the lab for starters."

"Extra observation," Chor-Zor ordered from behind his mask and a mod stepped forwards and sat at an empty console table which immediately came to life. The mod placed his laser-gun down on the floor beside his boots.

"Ready, sire," said the mod.

"There's really no need for him," Alice said.

"Continue," replied the Headmaster. "Let's go, please,

Banks."

"Well," Mr Banks said. "Whenever you're ready, then, Alice."

"I'm ready."

"Launching Nano."

"Headmaster, Pull-Mun, Row-Lin, report please."

All of them came back: "Clear."

"Safe journey, everyone."

The room was calm. Alice lay on her back staring through the eyepiece at the painting of Julius Caesar in Gaul, concentrating hard on the image. She knew little of the Roman period of history, nothing of the history of Gaul or Britain. If they'd asked her about the Moon, about how it had been formed from the Earth, or the first American missions, the first mines, the first permanent port – even the treaties and pioneers of the first years of the NLCs – she might have been able to give them something real. But Julius Caesar? *Nada.* The only thing she really knew was that Aunt Athy and Charlie were there – and that these three would be soon.

And she did have the brooch.

And as she pretended to concentrate on the painting, she rubbed it, and the chain, in her hand. *Work, little thing,* she thought. *Work, work.*

"I see something," Chor-Zor reported. His voice was higher than usual, tinged with excitement. In his visor he could see Alice's brain: soft and furry, suspended in pea soup.

Mr Banks: "Switch to shades. Follow the yellows."

"I see yellow!" Pull-Mun was excited. The new visuals were clearer: it was obvious where the ideas were forming. "I see it! A huge star forming – can you see it?"

"I see it!" Chor-Zor cried.

Row-Lin was tense, her purple-tipped nails threatening to scratch their way out of the gloves. "Yes! I see it too!"

A great, yellow galaxy-burst rose slowly out of a deep cavern in Alice's brain and began to swell in front of the Nani, large on the mods' screens.

"Dive for it!" Chor-Zor said, his hands automatically coming up to protect his eyes: the light seemed so close and real. "Get it! That must be it!"

"Fire!" ordered Row-Lin, desperate.

"Fire! Fire!" shouted Pull-Mun.

Mr Banks fired the Nani's javelins and couldn't miss. "Hit!" His voice was neither happy nor sad. "You're locked on. That was a direct hit."

Alice's body spasmed as the idea took hold. She was asleep now, in REM sleep, dreaming, thinking, and the three mods were also still, flat and immobile, fully connected to her and the idea. While they remained attached to the machine and the idea, the mods were as good as frozen.

Mr Banks felt a tap on his shoulder and turned, angry, expecting to find a mod or one of Chor-Zor's henchmen but instead he saw Charlie dripping with water. In the doorway behind Charlie were three mods lying on the floor, face down. The mod who'd been put on extra observation was slumped over his console. Charlie had stolen his stun-stick. "Howdy," Charlie said.

Mr Banks was wide-eyed. "Vonnegut? Is it really you? What's going on?"

"Let 'em go," Charlie said quietly. When Mr Banks pulled a surprised face, Charlie drew his fingers across his throat. "I know what Alice is doing. I've seen them there – they arrived!" he hissed. "Let them go!"

For the first time in a long time, Mr Banks smiled. "Aye, aye." He turned back to his controls, flipped his mask down and said: "Ejecting Nano."

Chor-Zor might have heard something but he was already on the boat, crossing the Channel, under one of the huge orange sails.

He, Row-Lin and Pull-Mun had just seen Charlie wading out from the beach.

XXVIII

Old England
The distant past

Chor-Zor waited with his spear held high but the boy didn't resurface.

Row-Lin and Pull-Mun, also in full military uniform, looked down into the foamy sea. "Where is he?" Chor-Zor asked. He jabbed at the fizzing spume with the sharp point of the spear.

"Soldiers! Prepare for landing!"

There was little Row-Lin, Pull-Mun and Chor-Zor could do but fall into line. Their boat was close to the shore and the soldiers who'd disembarked before them looked to have cleared the beach. Their own boat got close enough into the shingle shore that long planks were thrown down meaning none of them wet their feet as they ran ashore.

Eagle standards fluttered from the tops of the cliffs, and helmets and shields glinted against the white cliff faces where the advance forces were zigzagging their way to the top.

"This is too real now, sire," Row-Lin said, walking across to stand with Chor-Zor. The mods were the last three soldiers on the beach. Each found it difficult to manage real, human limbs and walk on sand.

Chor-Zor, his face morphed convincingly into that of a soldier's, complete with scar, touched the side of his head where the earpiece should have been. "This is too sharp on the senses, Banks! Bring us back immediately."

All of them turned in horror as Pull-Mun, who in this world had a long, red beard, suddenly yelled in pain and fell sideways on to the grey rocks and pebbles. From up on a hillside there was a shout of pride: a blue-skinned savage was jumping up and down, celebrating.

"What's going on here?" Chor-Zor asked. He was very aware

that they were alone and exposed now.

Row-Lin was a sharp-faced woman, thin and muscular, with plaited brown hair and bad skin. She looked scared. "I think we should go back." And then, in total disbelief and horror: "I think Mr Pull-Mun is *bleeding*, sire."

"Leave him!" a passing Roman captain shouted. "Press on! Press on!"

Chor-Zor pressed his ear. "Bring us back, Banks. Abort mission. Now!"

"Bring us back," Row-Lin repeated, angrily. She ducked as a fresh shower of catapulted rocks came raining down upon them.

The savages were only to be seen on one hill now, racing backwards and forwards in chariots, screaming obscenities at the top of their lungs. Some Roman artillery had been assembled on nearby clifftops and their fire began streaming through the darkening sky.

"Nothing," said Chor-Zor.

He and Row-Lin pulled Pull-Mun up.

"Something's gone wrong, sire," Row-Lin said aloud. She couldn't allow herself to think about what might be happening: that they had been cut loose in a real-life version of a painting on the wall of the school, cut loose in ancient history. As they struggled along, she placed a hand on her ear and shouted: "Bring us back right now and that's an order!"

The rope netting which flew over her, Chor-Zor and Pull-Mun's heads was so heavy it knocked Row-Lin off her feet. Chor-Zor somehow remained standing and swung his spear about for the few moments it took for the gang of local ruffians to jump on top of the net. There were six boys in the gang, all Britons, and they yelped with delight as they felt the two bodies struggling in their net. Rachlan was standing guard nearby with a small knife keeping an eye out for Romans.

Chor-Zor was whipped on to his side and grabbed the netting as he and Row-Lin were dragged like a catch of fish up the pebble beach by the gang. No shouting or threatening worked and their weapons were taken through the rough rope.

Chor-Zor tried to look back at the boats and sea but it was the first time in his life he'd ever been exposed to "fresh" air and the filthiness of it overpowered him. As if the smell of the sea and salt and fish was not bad enough, the boys pulling them along stunk like wild animals. The stench was pure dirt.

The sea air had the same effect on Row-Lin: it made her feel sleepy and drowsy. She was also coming to terms with the fact that she had real limbs – those fingers she could see whitening at the knuckles were really hers, connected to her. The cold she could feel was real cold. The pain, real pain. When she was very young she had thought about this. About what it must be like to be human. But she had been weak then.

They found themselves in a cave, and Rachlan and the others wouldn't let them out of the net until they'd surrendered all their weapons and armour to the gang. Only then did Rachlan and the other yobs leave them, and when they'd gone, the three mods-turned-humans sat in their threadbare underwear on the sharp, black rocks near the cave edge, looking mournfully out at the rough sea.

"Hello again," came a voice from behind them.

All turned to see Mrs Jull-Costa standing in the darkness of the cave tunnel. She was dressed in white robes which danced out behind her in the sea wind.

"You?" asked Chor-Zor, incredulously. He stood up, shivering, his long, matted hair blowing up on his head.

"Me," Athy replied, nodding.

"You will get us out of here and back to St Francis' right this instant!" Pull-Mun shouted, one hand over his bleeding cheek. The blood had dried black in his beard and he was spitting with fury. "This is all your fault, you thief!"

"I will do nothing of the sort," Athy replied.

"How dare you speak to us like this?" Row-Lin asked. She

was hissing, too, though careful to keep her footing on the sharp rocks. Waves came rolling in and burst over the rocks at the cave entrance. The sea was getting rougher as the day went on.

"Now it looks as though you will learn what it is to be human," Athy told them. She stepped down off the rock she was standing on into a small patch of sand. "With all its imperfections."

"Witch!" Pull-Mun shouted.

"Wait!" Chor-Zor replied. Ever the diplomat, he held out a hand to Athy and said: "All right. We have learned our lesson. I don't understand the methods you have used to trap us here, but, on behalf of all of us, I accept that you have won."

"You murdered my friend, Ma'am Mallowan."

"I..." but Chor-Zor had no answer.

"You started this," Athy continued, walking past the three of them towards the crashing grey waves. "I will leave you with some advice. This cave leads to a system which stretches back far underground and there are good people here, living in the cave. Use your new-found humanity and make peace with them, make friends. Make the most of your time here."

"Where are you going?" asked Row-Lin, nervousness in her voice as she watched the old woman begin to walk into the high waves.

"I'm going home," Athy replied.

The mods watched as the waves engulfed her and she seemed to vanish right before their eyes. Pull-Mun was too weak, but Chor-Zor and Row-Lin ran towards the beach, stopping at the shore line, where the waves came in.

"She disappeared," Chor-Zor said. "Like the boy."

"Disappeared when she entered the waves," agreed Row-Lin.

"It is some kind of witchcraft."

"Magic," agreed Row-Lin.

"Oh, Ma'am Mallowan," Chor-Zor said, looking up at the dark clouds. "You are really something."

"Shall we too go into the water?" asked Row-Lin, looking out at the sea. There were some soldiers still in the boats. A single vessel was on fire, crackling in the rain.

"First we take care of him," Chor-Zor replied, turning to look at poor Pull-Mun who was lying on his side in the sand. "And then we make a decision together."

XXIX

The Future

"This must be it." Charlie pulled the neck of his suit over his nose as he pulled up the hatch's sticky handle. He'd thrown back the hairy black and white sheet which had been on top of the sofa and was kneeling on the sticky floor. Alice was standing nearby, eyes watering, gagging.

Romulus and Remus mewled and purred as Charlie bent shoulder deep into the hole.

"Yes!" Charlie looked back at his sister and clenched his free fist. Alice stepped forward and saw there was something in the hole, a package wrapped in Mrs Mallowan's scarlet funeral cloth. Charlie lifted the bundle and quickly unravelled it: it was an old, battered, rectangular object. "Is this it?" he asked. Alice stared back and shrugged.

"Is there anything else in there?" asked Alice.

Charlie pressed his fingers around the empty spaces in the cubbyhole. "No. This has to be it. It's exactly where Aunty Athy said it would be." He looked up at her. "Is this a book?"

Alice shrugged. "Maybe? What does one look like?"

Charlie turned the heavy red rectangle one way and then the other and managed, finally, to reveal two heavy, dry, yellowed pages covered with scrawled writing. "Yes! See! That's it! That's writing! Aunt Athy told me – this *is* a book!"

"Pages!" shouted Alice suddenly, pointing, clapping and skipping. "That's what Granny Red used to call them! Pages!"

"I need a pen!" Charlie said.

Alice nodded but then stopped and asked: "What's a pen?"

"It's a kind of stick," Charlie said, rolling his hands. "It makes marks in these things. Aunt Athy said there might be one in here." The flat was a foul mess. The cats hadn't been out in days, and the food their aunt had left behind had gone rotten.

Some of the old floorboards had begun to warp and there were green patches of mould on the walls. *Aunt Athy turned the heating up in here*, Charlie had thought when they'd first entered. *She wanted it to be like this!*

"Are you sure there's nothing in the hole?"

Charlie looked down again, grimaced, dived in and fumbled about. Romulus jumped on to his wrist and Charlie yelled out in frustration. "Oh, why didn't I ask her where it would be?"

"Wait," Alice said. She knelt beside Charlie. "Look."

The Book itself was old and leather-bound, reddish, a kind of faded cherry colour. Next to it, where Alice was pointing, stuck to the floorboards, being gently kicked by Remus' black and white paw, he saw a thin, black instrument which looked like a magic wand. It must have rolled out of the pages when they'd opened it.

"Of course," Charlie said aloud, nodding. "Thanks, Aunt Athy!"

"They've gone into a panic," Roald told Alice. "Apparently Chor-Zor, Pull-Mun and Row-Lin have vanished and the remaining mods and cyborgs are having a meeting now in the dome to try and work out what to do. There's no protocol for this so imagine how confused they are."

"How are the humans?" Alice was sitting on the top landing outside her aunt's flat, speaking into one of the security suits she'd taken from a cupboard on the same landing.

"As far as we know they're all right. They're still down in the cells. I'm not sure how they're doing for food, air or water but as far as I know they're all in there and all still alive."

"Do you think you can get into that cell?" Alice asked.

"Which cell? Where they are?" Roald nodded. "Yes, why not. It's a standard seal."

"I want you and Aurora to go there."

"Alice! They've tracked this message. I can see they have a

trace on it."

"Roald, listen to me. Here's what I want you to do…"

Charlie, back in his aunt's flat, shirt pulled up over his mouth, wrote what Aunt Athy had told him to write in The Book and knelt up on his haunches.

He'd half-expected a *shazam!* moment: perhaps some smoke and lightning, but nothing happened. Romulus and Remus padded about him, nosy as ever, and noisy too, and now his sister appeared in the doorway. "Did you do it?"

"Yep. But – nothing."

"But did you do *exactly* what Aunt Athy asked you to do?"

"Yes!" Charlie shook his head. "Obviously."

"Well, then, let's go. Wrap the book up, grab a cat, and let's get out of here."

"Where are we going?"

"Home," said Alice.

"Home?"

"You take Romulus, I take Remus." Alice led Charlie back down the corridor to the cupboard and told him to put on a protection suit. "Put your cat in your jacket. There's an inside pocket. Pass me that while you get changed."

"Alice. What's going on?" asked Charlie. He peered down over the bannisters at the main hall and saw it was empty.

"I just told you," Alice replied. "We're going home. Now put your suit on and hurry up. The mods are coming and they're not happy."

XXX

Deep below the dome, the cell door opened and the sight and smell which greeted Roald and Aurora made their eyes water.

All the human teachers and students were crowded together, lying in huddles or alone, groaning with hunger and sadness. Some raised their hands or cried out about the "bright" light from the doorway.

"Please come with us," Aurora said. "Please try and get to your feet and come with us."

"We're here to save you!" Roald shouted, clapping his hands and moving along the first line of bodies. "Come on! Get up! Let's get out of here!"

The humans looked scared. "Where?" one asked, so emaciated Roald didn't recognise her.

"Where are you taking us? Can't you let us stay here. That door is giving a draught."

"We're going somewhere safe," Roald told them. "You have to trust us. We've been sent here by Mrs Jull-Costa. She's organised an escape for you all but you must move now. It's not far."

Something in his voice roused the weak hordes and they began getting up, helping each other, and soon they were streaming out of the vault, hobbling, arm in arm. There was no rush and no pushing and nobody was left behind.

XXXI

Alice and Charlie ran out of the main entrance of the school as three mods came up the tunnel from the dome. As Alice had hoped, the mods stopped at the protective seal and awaited orders. Looking back she saw them standing there, dark mannequins behind the bubble-like invisible wall. The devil in her made her wave.

"Seriously, Alice, don't annoy them. You're nuts sometimes." Charlie was nervous about Romulus, who was struggling inside his suit. If the cat's claws pierced the material, this was over. "Please tell me you know where we're going."

"To the lawn," Alice replied, panting, pointing ahead. "Jump over the little wall. Watch the flower beds – the stumps are dangerous. That's it. Keep running. Don't stop!"

"This cat stinks!"

Looking ahead, Charlie got a shock as he saw Aunt Athy standing like a ghost in the pale brown air on the far side of the black lawn. She wore no protection suit, was dressed all in white and was dripping with water. It made her look as though she were a ghost, shining with jewels or heavenly light.

Charlie checked his valves and readings – something must have got into his air. He was seeing things. The blood pumped hard in his ears. When Aunt Athy waved at him, her figure moving back and forth in the thick, woozy atmosphere, it felt like the end. *I'm dying*, he thought.

Alice was more concerned about their great-aunt's breathing. As soon as she reached Athy she took off her mask and let the old lady gulp the air.

"Thank you," Athy croaked. She was glad to be back, to see the old school again. Her spirits were raised when she saw the cats' heads poking up from inside the children's suits. Romulus and Remus recognised her and mewled.

"Good to see you, Aunty," Charlie panted as he arrived. He turned to the Main Building, hands on his knees, fighting for breath. "I'll go back for another suit." This plan was immediately nixed by the sight of six mods streaming out of the main entrance in dark protective suits, all armed.

"Stay here, Charlie," Athy said. "Alice, take some air."

Alice did as she was told and she, Charlie and Athy stood at the edge of the darkened black square as the mods jumped the small wall between them.

Charlie glanced at the sharp trunks of the trees behind them and wondered if he could maybe, somehow, make a weapon of any of them but there was something in him that knew it was too late. Besides, the mods had weapons. There were six of them. This was a step too far.

"Stay calm," Athy said. "Share the air."

It was Alice who noticed the abjads first.

The mods were too busy closing in on their prey to notice that it was they who were being hunted. The glowing, wrinkled abjads darted out of the ruined buildings half-hidden in the dirty day. As the mods began to arrow in on Alice, Charlie and Aunt Athy – ordering them to put their hands up – the abjads struck from their blindsides, leaping three each on every mod and sucking at the power sources on their backs. For a moment there was a squeal of feedback-like noise and then the mods arched their backs in pain. They collapsed with the abjads on them, white gargoyles feeding, and all was silent. More abjads came skipping out of the brown fog to feed on the fallen.

"Your turn, Aunt," Alice said, passing her the air piece.

As Aunt Athy took a breath she noticed what she'd thought was a cloud above her head moving. It was something solid, silver, descending. A fierce, warm wind blew down upon their heads and, inside the protective suits, Romulus and Remus clawed with fear.

Charlie's suit tore open with the downward thrust and he

breathed a mouthful of toxic air but the huge cruiser was almost down now, and Roald's face became visible through one of the small now-materialising windows high up in the clear shell.

A door appeared and opened lower down, steps unravelled, and four human figures in suits ran out and grabbed Charlie, Alice and Athy.

In the cockpit they all watched the brownish Earth become a dull, grey marble and Charlie coughed and nudged Aurora as Roald set a course for the New Lunar Colonies. "I promised you I'd take you home," he told her, winking.

Aurora laughed. "I don't know how you managed it, Charlie Vonnegut – but, you know what? I don't care!"

"They're asking for the name of the ship," Roald told everyone, a finger on his earpiece. They had the Moon in their sights.

"*The Cat*," said Aunt Athy, stroking a very contented Romulus and Remus.

"And our destination?" Roald asked.

"First the New Lunar Colonies," Aunt Athy said, nodding towards Aurora. "And then on to the Fourth for some family business." She smiled at Alice and Charlie. "After that," she concluded, laying a hand on Roald's shoulder. "Whoever wants to stay about and go hunting big blue exoplanets is more than welcome to do so."

"I'm just glad the tennis courts were soft enough," Alice told Roald when they were finally alone. "That was the only thing I was really worried about."

"The earth disintegrated like dust," Roald replied. "Luckily."

In front of them they could see the shimmering settlements of the New Lunar Colonies. Ashy domes dotted the surface while low-gravity cruisers zipped about like lurid, mechanised dragonflies. Aurora was looking down with a tear in her eye. "I'd love to see your home," she said to Charlie. "Mars. All of that."

"Then come," he replied. "We can wait for you."

"I couldn't do that!"

"Why not?" Charlie shrugged. "We've got all the time in the world now. Maybe your dad would want to come?"

"I'll ask him," Aurora replied, eyes wet. "I'll ask him."

Athy put down the oxygen mask she'd been using and walked out of the cockpit area, through to the main hall. It was good to see and hear such a bright, happy atmosphere there now: the humans were eating, drinking and resting – all in great spirits. As she walked across the lounge Sam Cauldhame came lumbering over and they embraced gently.

"We're getting old, Sam," Athy said.

"You are," replied Sam. He smiled at her. "Do I have you to thank for all this?"

"Oh, no. This is all Kizzie's doing."

"How so?"

"Let me show you. Call Leana."

Athy led Sam and Leana to her small cabin, not far from the main area. There was a bed and small window full of dark sky and stars. Laid on the white bedsheets was The Book. "Kizzie was worried about the school, you see. About the spirit of the school. That's what all this was about."

"What happens to St Francis' now, then?" asked Sam, touching the red cover. Leana was beside him, holding his hand.

"Oh, it goes on, Sam. While The Book is here, it goes on." Athy mentioned Roald. "That's Agatha's grandson flying this contraption, you know. Says he's always had a dream about a blue planet. Says he would love to find one." She raised an eyebrow. "Blue planets go well with schools, eh?"

"Squaring the circle, too?" Sam replied, cryptically.

"Perhaps. Perhaps."

"The plan is to fly right out of the solar system then, is it?" Leana asked, looking out of the window at the brown, smudged marble of the Earth. "Makes a change from travelling into the past, I suppose."

"Oh, I don't think I'll be going with them all the way out there," Athy said. "I'd like to spend some time with Kizzie. Catch up. Be calm. Think about the past, perhaps." Athy touched Sam's back. "And you two?"

Sam shook his fleshy jowls. "Oh, you know, I think we might both like to see how the story ends. Or starts again, whichever it may be."

"That could be interesting," agreed Leana. "I like not knowing what's coming next."

"Life's a mystery story," Sam told her.

"It certainly is."

Athy nodded at them both. "And why not."

"You're not interested in knowing what happens next, Athy?" Leana asked.

"Oh, I'm quite sure all will be well in the end."

Sam scoffed. "And how can you be so sure, all of a sudden? You, who were always the shy one? Never sure of yourself?"

"Well," Athy replied, walking across to The Book and tapping the page Charlie had written on. "I've read it, haven't I?"

Sam and Leana leaned down, squinting, backs creaking, and read the swirling letters on the old, dry page:

And They All Lived Happily Ever After.

Caesar, according to his usual custom, happened to be signing his letters as he lay at table, when the conversation fell upon what was the best form of death.

Anticipating all the rest, Caesar exclaimed:

"The unexpected."

Plutarch's Lives

LODESTONE
BOOKS

YOUNG ADULT FICTION

Lodestone Books is a new imprint, which offers a broad spectrum of subjects in YA/NA literature. Compelling reading, the Teen/Young/New Adult reader is sure to find something edgy, enticing and innovative. From dystopian societies, through a whole range of fantasy, horror, science fiction and paranormal fiction, all the way to the other end of the sphere, historical drama, steam-punk adventure, and everything in between (including crime, coming of age and contemporary romance). Whatever your preference you will discover it here.
If you have enjoyed this book, why not tell other readers by posting a review on your preferred book site. Recent bestsellers from Lodestone Books are:

AlphaNumeric
Nicolas Forzy
When dyslexic teenager Stu accidentally transports himself into a world populated by living numbers and letters, his arrival triggers a prophecy that pulls two rival communities into war.
Paperback: 978-1-78279-506-3 ebook: 978-1-78279-505-6

Time Sphere
A timepathway book
M.C. Morison
When a teenage priestess in Ancient Egypt connects with a school-boy on a visit to the British Museum, they each come under threat as they search for Time's Key.
Paperback: 978-1-78279-330-4 ebook: 978-1-78279-329-8

Bird Without Wings
FAEBLES
Cally Pepper
Sixteen-year-old Scarlett has had more than her fair share of problems, but nothing prepares her for the day she discovers she's growing wings...
Paperback: 978-1-78099-902-9 ebook: 978-1-78099-901-2

Briar Blackwood's Grimmest of Fairytales
Timothy Roderick
After discovering she is the fabled Sleeping Beauty, a brooding goth-girl races against time to undo her deadly fate.
Paperback: 978-1-78279-922-1 ebook: 978-1-78279-923-8

Escape from the Past
The Duke's Wrath
Annette Oppenlander
Trying out an experimental computer game, a fifteen-year-old boy unwittingly time-travels to medieval Germany where he must not only survive but figure out a way home.
Paperback: 978-1-84694-973-9 ebook: 978-1-78535-002-3

Holding On and Letting Go
K.A. Coleman
When her little brother died, Emerson's life came crashing down around her. Now she's back home and her friends want to help, but can Emerson fight to re-enter the world she abandoned?
Paperback: 978-1-78279-577-3 ebook: 978-1-78279-576-6

Midnight Meanders
Annika Jensen
As William journeys through his own mind, revelations are made, relationships are broken and restored, and a faith that once seemed extinct is renewed.
Paperback: 978-1-78279-412-7 ebook: 978-1-78279-411-0

Reggie & Me
The First Book in the Dani Moore Trilogy
Marie Yates
The first book in the Dani Moore Trilogy, *Reggie & Me* explores a teenager's search for normalcy in the aftermath of rape.
Paperback: 978-1-78279-723-4 ebook: 978-1-78279-722-7

Unconditional
Kelly Lawrence
She's in love with a boy from the wrong side of town...
Paperback: 978-1-78279-394-6 ebook: 978-1-78279-393-9

Readers of ebooks can buy or view any of these bestsellers by clicking on the live link in the title. Most titles are published in paperback and as an ebook. Paperbacks are available in traditional bookshops. Both print and ebook formats are available online.

Find more titles and sign up to our readers' newsletter at
http://www.johnhuntpublishing.com/children-and-young-adult
Follow us on Facebook at
https://www.facebook.com/JHPChildren
and Twitter at
https://twitter.com/JHPChildren